DOCTOR WHO AND THE
DALEK INVASION OF EARTH

Kevin Lourage
60 Royston Lane
Royston
Barnsley
South Yorkshire
S71 4PL

DOCTOR WHO
AND THE DALEK
INVASION OF EARTH

Based on the BBC television serial *Doctor Who and the World's End* by Terry Nation by arrangement with the British Broadcasting Corporation

TERRANCE DICKS

A TARGET BOOK

published by
the *Paperback Division of*
W. H. ALLEN & Co. Ltd

A Target Book
Published in 1977
by the Paperback Division of W. H. Allen & Co. Ltd
A Howard & Wyndham Company
123 King Street, London W6 9JG

Published simultaneously in Great Britain by
Allan Wingate (Publishers) Ltd, 1977

Printed in Great Britain by
Richard Clay (The Chaucer Press) Ltd, Bungay, Suffolk

ISBN 0 426 11244 X

Contents

Return to Terror

Through the ruin of a city stalked the ruin of a man. His clothes were tattered and grimy, his skin blotched and diseased over wasted flesh. On his head was a gleaming metal helmet. He walked with the stiff, jerky movements of a robot—which was exactly what he had become.

The robot man moved through the shattered rubble of a once-great city, a fitting inhabitant of a nightmare landscape.

In time he came to a river, a sluggish, debris-choked, polluted stream which had once carried great ships. He quickened his pace, sensing that the water would provide the thing he sought—a way to end an existence of misery and pain.

When he came to a gap in the embankment wall, he marched stiffly through it and plunged into the water below. He fell, like a log or a stone, making no attempt to save himself. Dragged down by the weight of the helmet, his head sank beneath the grimy waters. There was something inhuman about the manner of his death—but then, he had not been truly human for a very long time.

Not far away, on the rubble-littered remains of what had been a building site, something very strange happened. There was a wheezing, groaning sound and suddenly a square blue police box materialised out of thin air, light flashing busily on top.

Inside the police box, things were stranger still. There was a large, brightly lit, ultra-modern control room. In the centre was a many-sided control panel, its surfaces covered with a complex array of knobs, switches, levers and dials. From the size of the control room it was clear that the police box must be bigger on the inside than on the outside.

Around the centre console stood an oddly-assorted group of people.

The oldest was a man who appeared to be somewhere in his sixties, though in reality he was very much older. He wore check trousers, a frock-coat and a long black tie. He had flowing white hair and a proud, imperious face, with more than a touch of ruthless cunning.

The three others were more ordinary in appearance. There was a young man and a young woman, both somewhere in their twenties, and a dark pretty girl in her teens. All three were casually dressed in the clothes worn on Earth in the last part of the twentieth century.

The young man was called Ian Chesterton, the woman Barbara Wright. Once, though it seemed a very long time ago, they had both been schoolteachers. Led by their curiosity about Susan, the youngest member of the party, then one of their pupils, they had followed her home. To their amazement, they had discovered that she appeared to live in this police box with a mysterious old man known only as the Doctor, who she said was her grandfather. They had been even more astonished to find themselves inside the police box, and to discover that it was a kind of Space/Time ship, called the TARDIS—a name formed from the

8

initial letters of Time and Relative Dimensions In Space.

Then had begun a series of terrifying journeys through Time and Space. The TARDIS had many extraordinary qualities, but accuracy of steering did not appear to be one of them. The Doctor's attempts to return them to their own time and place resulted only in an incredible number of unplanned arrivals, sometimes on alien planets, sometimes on Earth, though always at completely the wrong period. They had seen many wonders, and undergone many strange adventures. Such is the adaptability of the human spirit that they had now adjusted to a life of Space/Time travel. Though they still hoped to see twentieth century Earth again, their old life had begun to seem more and more like a kind of dream.

Now the TARDIS had made yet another landing. They were all waiting with mingled anticipation and apprehension to discover what lay ahead this time. Moreover, to the Doctor's extreme annoyance, they were all being rather sceptical about his assurances that they were back on Earth, and in the twentieth century.

'Let's take a look on the scanner,' suggested Ian practically.

The Doctor switched on, and they all peered into the viewing screen. The picture was dark and fuzzy, like an old TV set in a poor reception area. 'Oh dear, oh dear, it's not clear,' said the Doctor peevishly. 'It's not clear at all.' He glared at them accusingly, as if it were all their fault.

'I wonder where we really are,' said Ian thoughtfully.

Barbara sighed. 'Somewhere quiet and peaceful, I hope.' She knew from bitter experience that the TARDIS never seemed to take them anywhere *safe*.

Susan gave her a quick smile. 'Yes, we could all do with a holiday, couldn't we?'

Barbara peered at the murk on the scanner. 'I can't see *anything*.'

Ian looked over her shoulder. 'Don't worry, neither can I!'

The Doctor indicated sluggish movement on the screen. 'That could be water. A river, perhaps.' Ian gave him a sceptical look, and the Doctor turned away in a huff. 'Susan, perhaps you'll be kind enough to give me the instrument readings?'

Susan was already studying dials on one of the control panels. 'Radiation nil, oxygen and air pressure normal.'

'Normal for *where*?' snapped the Doctor. He hated any kind of imprecision, especially in matters of science.

'Normal for Earth, grandfather,' said Susan excitedly. 'This is a typical Earth reading.'

The Doctor gave a self-satisfied sniff, as if he'd known the answer all along. 'I don't want to boast, my friends,' he said loftily, 'but that might well be London out there!'

Ian and Barbara exchanged rueful looks. In theory the Doctor's words were true enough. It might indeed be twentieth-century London out there. But on his previous record, it might equally well be some savage alien planet—or the Earth of some completely different age.

Ian braced himself. 'Well, what are we waiting for? Let's go and take a look.'

Barbara agreed. 'Doctor, open the door, please. We'll chance it!'

For a moment the Doctor continued to look sulky. Then he gave one of his sudden charming smiles. 'Yes, of course, my dear.'

He touched the controls, the door swung open, and they all went outside.

They found themselves in an open area, surrounded by high buildings. In front the ground sloped down towards a wide river. There were scattered piles of building material all around, bricks, timber, steel girders in enormous stacks. Many of the stacks were partially collapsed—the one nearest the TARDIS was in a particularly perilous state.

There was an ironic gleam in the Doctor's eye as he looked at Chesterton. 'Well, here you are, my boy—home at last. There's the Thames.'

'We've come a pretty roundabout way, Doctor.'

The Doctor nodded. 'And arrived more by luck than judgement,' he said, with one of his disarming flashes of honesty. He looked distastefully at the rubble all around. 'This is a pretty horrible mess, isn't it?'

Barbara nodded in agreement. It wasn't a particularly pretty spot to choose for a homecoming. But at least it was Earth.

'Where do you think we are, Ian?'

'Looks like a building-site, down by the Docks. It all seems pretty deserted. We can follow the river into central London, there'll be people about there.'

Ian and Barbara began making plans to find their homes and friends again. The Doctor watched them, frowning. He ran his hand along the nearest girder, then inspected it. His fingers were covered in thick rust. The Doctor's frown deepened. Building material was valuable. You didn't leave it out in the open to decay unused.

'I wonder which year we're in,' he muttered.

Ian caught the worried tone. 'What's the matter, Doctor?'

'Eh? Oh, I was just worrying about the time factor, my boy.'

'After all our travels, we're not going to quibble about a year here or there!'

The Doctor sniffed. For all their recent experiences, these young people didn't realise the dangers and paradoxes in time travel. Suppose they met their own grandparents while they were still children? Or worse still, arrived at a time when all their family and friends were already dead? He kept these gloomy thoughts to himself and said, 'For both your sakes, I hope we're very near to your own time. But bear in mind, we may have arrived in the early nineteen hundreds—or in the twenty-fifth century!'

Barbara refused to be downhearted. 'Well, it's still London. No mistaking that, I can feel it in the air,' she said cheerfully.

Suddenly they realised Susan was no longer with them. She'd grown bored with the conversation of her elders, and slipped away. Ian hunted round for her unsuccessfully. Then it occurred to him to look up. Sure enough Susan was far above their heads, scrambling up the pile of girders. 'What do you think you're doing?' he yelled.

'Just having a look around. Can't see a thing from down there.'

Ian was about to order her down when he was distracted by the Doctor, who said mysteriously, *'Decay!'*

Ian and Barbara stared at him. The Doctor went on talking as if to himself. 'That's the word I was looking for—decay!'

Barbara put a hand on his arm. 'Doctor, what's worrying you?'

'Look at all this! Preparations for some great constructional work. A new bridge across the river, perhaps. Not a small undertaking. Yet all around us is this air of neglect. This place has been *abandoned*—and for quite some time too.'

Ian could see the force of the Doctor's arguments, but he didn't want to admit, even to himself, that the Doctor might be right. The thought that perhaps they weren't home safely after all was too awful to be faced. 'There's always a lot of mess in construction work, Doctor,' he said unconvincingly.

The Doctor was staring into space, his mind trying to solve the problem on the little evidence available. 'Perhaps, my boy, perhaps,' he murmured. 'And yet . . .'

Barbara shivered. Like Ian, she didn't want her hopes of a safe return snatched away. 'Doctor, you're spoiling it all.'

The Doctor's keen glance went from one to the other of them. 'I'm sorry, my dear. The last thing I want to do is spoil your homecoming. But I think we ought to be wary . . .'

Susan's voice floated down from above. 'I'm nearly at the top now. Still can't see much, though. I'll just go a bit higher . . .'

Enjoying her own daring, Susan continued upwards. Suddenly the girder beneath her feet rocked a little. Nervously she said, 'Oops!'

But the girder steadied again. She worked her way along it and on to the very top of the pile. Balanced precariously, she stared at the view below in shocked disbelief.

Although she wasn't a native of Earth, Susan had lived there with the Doctor for quite some time. She was very familiar with the way that London ought to look. The sight of the deserted, half-ruined city came as as big a shock to her as it would have done to Ian or Barbara.

Susan wondered when they must have arrived. Somewhere in the nineteen-forties, perhaps? She knew London had been damaged in World War Two—but she couldn't remember hearing that the damage was as bad as this ... And how was she going to break the news to Ian and Barbara?

She heard Ian calling. 'Susan, be careful! What's it like up there?'

'Doesn't seem to be anyone about,' she called back. 'And the whole city's ...' The girder beneath her feet twisted sideways, and Susan lost her footing. She made a desperate grab at the nearest girder but her hand slipped, and she began a bumpy slide down the side of the pile.

The others looked on horrified and helpless, as she tumbled from the pile, landing almost at their feet. Barbara ran to her, kneeling by her side. Susan stirred and muttered, 'Ruined ... all ruined,' then fell back unconscious. Barbara felt her head with skilful hands. There was a slight trickle of blood on Susan's forehead.

'She grazed her head on the way down but there doesn't seem to be any real injury. She'll be all right.'

The Doctor looked down at Susan, disguising his very real concern with an air of irritation. 'She will go dashing about,' he said disapprovingly—forgetting that he spent his whole life in dashing about on a far greater scale.

Ian helped Barbara to sit Susan up. 'Daft kid,' he grumbled, sounding very much like the schoolteacher he'd once been. 'She's lucky it wasn't worse——'

The Doctor rested a hand on the nearest girder. It was *vibrating*. 'I'm afraid it is worse,' he said urgently. 'That pile was finely balanced, and Susan disturbed the equilibrium.'

They stared upwards and saw a huge steel girder,

balanced see-saw like across another, tilt slowly to one side. There was a rumbling, grinding sound as the whole pile began to shift. Susan's fall, though minor in itself, had been like the shout that starts an avalanche…

'The whole lot's going,' yelled Ian. 'Let's get out of here!'

The Doctor had already spotted the only safe shelter —the arched doorway of a half-completed building nearby. 'Come on,' he called. 'Over here!' Dragging Susan between them, Ian and Barbara followed him.

From beneath the shelter of the archway they watched the collapse of the pile of girders. It was an impressive spectacle, accompanied by an ear-splitting clang of metal and clouds of dust.

The last girder clattered to the ground and there was a deafening silence. Coughing and choking, the Doctor peered out. 'Everybody all right? Splendid!' He seemed rather exhilarated by the adventure.

'We're all right,' said Ian. 'What about the TARDIS?'

The Doctor smiled complacently. 'How many times must I tell you, Chesterton, my boy, the TARDIS is indestructible.'

The dust was settling now, and the Doctor left the shelter of the arch and began making his way towards the TARDIS. Suddenly he called in an alarmed voice. 'The Ship, Chesterton, the Ship!'

Ian ran to join him, then stopped in horror. The police box was still visible—but only just. An impenetrable tangle of twisted steel girders blocked the way to its entrance. The TARDIS was safe right enough—but they couldn't get back inside it.

2

The Roboman

The Doctor began tugging crossly at one of the obstructing girders. Ian came to help him, but they were wasting their strength. Ian shrugged and gave up, stepping back and wiping his hands. 'We'll need help to shift this lot, Doctor. We'd better try and find someone.'

The Doctor didn't move. He stood gazing at the twisted pile of wreckage, rubbing his chin thoughtfully. 'Remember where we are, Chesterton.'

'We're in London—oh, yes, I see what you mean. Why do we want to get into a police box, people will ask.'

'Ironic, isn't it?' The Doctor was still studying the wreckage. 'Now as I see it, this girder here is the main problem. Shift that and we could open the door of the Ship far enough to squeeze inside.'

Ian looked at the girder. Luckily it was thinner than the rest. 'I could cut through it with an oxy-acetylene torch.'

'Easier said than done, my boy. One can't just whistle up machinery and tools at a moment's notice.' The Doctor looked at Ian with an infuriating air of expectancy. His manner suggested that he already had the answer to the problem, and was waiting to see if Ian could work it out for himself. Since Ian had a shrewd suspicion that the Doctor had no idea what to do next, he found this attitude particularly annoying. Ian glanced about him. 'That building over there looks like a warehouse of some kind. We might find something in it. Even a few crowbars would be a help.'

The Doctor shook his head disappointedly, like a teacher whose favourite pupil had let him down. 'I'm impressed by your optimism, my boy. But brute strength will never move that girder. No, a cutting flame is the right answer.'

Ian's temper boiled over. 'I'm sure of one thing, Doctor,' he snapped. 'We won't achieve anything just standing here. And we must be able to get into the TARDIS before we start looking round—just in case we run into trouble.'

The Doctor was quite unruffled. 'Good, good, Chesterton,' he said approvingly. 'A very intelligent observation.' Clearly the favourite pupil was doing better. Ian opened his mouth for a sharp retort, when the Doctor lowered his voice and led him a little further from the two girls. 'I have a feeling, Chesterton, an intuition if you like, that we're not in your time.'

A wave of disappointment swept over Ian, all the stronger because he himself shared the Doctor's suspicions. 'Just a feeling, Doctor?' he asked, hoping against hope.

The Doctor shook his head. 'Consider this, my boy. Here we are by the Thames. We've been here some little while. And what have we heard? Nothing. No sound of birdsong, no voices, no shipping, not even the chimes of Big Ben. Just an uncanny silence.'

Suddenly Ian realised the truth of the Doctor's words. Apart from the noises they'd made themselves, there'd been nothing but dead silence. Now deeply worried, he followed the Doctor back to the two girls.

Susan was trying to stand up, with Barbara supporting her. 'Ow, my foot!' She sank to the ground, looking apprehensively up at the Doctor. 'Sorry about what happened.'

The Doctor sniffed, showing no signs of his relief that Susan wasn't badly hurt. 'Oh, you're sitting up and taking notice, are you?'

'There don't seem to be any bones broken,' said Barbara encouragingly. 'Just a bit of a sprain.'

Susan was still looking at the Doctor. 'Don't be angry. After all, there's no real harm done.'

'Oh isn't there? Just look at all this mess in front of the Ship. We can't get in.'

Susan looked as if she was about to burst into tears. Hurriedly Ian said, 'We're going to take a look at that warehouse over there, see if we can find some tools.'

Barbara looked worried. 'Can't we all go?'

Susan tried standing up again, then collapsed with a wince of pain. 'My ankle seems to have got worse. It's all swelling up.'

Ian said, 'I'm afraid that settles it. We'll be back as soon as we can.'

Unhappily Barbara watched Ian and the Doctor move away. She turned back to Susan, who was rolling down her sock. 'That ankle does look swollen, doesn't it? Can you move your toes?'

Susan gave an experimental wiggle. 'Yes, it's fine until I put my whole weight on it. I've just twisted it a bit, that's all.'

Barbara looked towards the river. 'Suppose I go and soak my handkerchief with water for a sort of compress? That might relieve it a bit.'

Susan was already struggling to her feet. 'You're not leaving me here alone, she said determinedly. 'Give me a hand and I can manage to walk.' She put her arm round Barbara's shoulders for support, and they started hobbling towards the water.

By the time they reached the embankment Susan was exhausted. They stopped at the head of some steps leading down to the water and sat on the ground to rest. Barbara looked around. 'It's all too quiet. No traffic . . . this isn't my time, Susan. It can't be.'

Susan managed a smile. 'Well, back to the TARDIS and off we go again—as soon as we can get the door open.' She saw the sadness in Barbara's face. 'I'm sorry you're not home again after all.' Then she added honestly. 'Sorry for you, but not for me. I suppose I'm selfish, wanting us all to stay together.'

Barbara gave her a consoling hug. 'No, of course not.'

Susan looked at the silently flowing river. 'I think this must be long after your time. We can't expect things to stay as they are. They have to change, don't they?'

'I suppose so,' said Barbara sadly. 'Maybe London's been abandoned. Or maybe they've just done away with noise altogether! You stay there, I'll go down and get some water.'

Barbara made her way down the steps to the river's edge, and took out her handkerchief. By laying face down and stretching her arm, she was just able to dip her handkerchief in the murky water. As she straightened up, something caught her eye, and she jumped back, shuddering.

The body of a man was floating face-down in the water. His clothes were tattered and grimy, and his body seemed thin and emaciated inside them. Some unhappy tramp who'd decided to end everything, thought Barbara—then she noticed the gleaming metal helmet clamped to his head. The body drifted slowly away downstream.

Barbara stood up, half-inclined to drop the water-

19

soaked handkerchief back in the river. But she told herself not to be silly and started climbing the steps.

She was still wondering whether to tell Susan what she'd seen when she reached the top. But there was no one to tell. Susan had vanished. Barbara gazed round wildly. Susan couldn't have walked off, not with that ankle. She must have been *taken*. Suddenly she sensed a flicker of movement behind. Before she could react, a large, grimy hand clamped over her mouth, and she felt herself being dragged away ...

The Doctor and Ian had to go round the back of the warehouse before they found an unlocked door. It creaked open to reveal a flight of steps leading upwards into darkness. 'I'll go first, Doctor,' said Ian firmly. He led the way up the stairs. 'Keep close behind me—and be careful.'

He heard the Doctor's cross voice behind him. 'I'm not a half-wit, you know, Chesterton.' Ian smiled to himself. It would do the Doctor good to be treated like a child—a taste of his own medicine.

Halfway up the stairs Ian paused and called, 'Hallo! Hallo ... anybody there?' His voice echoed in the silence and he went on climbing. The staircase led to a long gloomy landing broken up with several doors. The nearest one, on their right, stood invitingly open, and Ian and the Doctor moved inside. (Intent on what was ahead of them, neither noticed when a door further down the corridor was pushed slightly ajar by a cautious hand. Through the crack, someone was watching them.)

They found themselves in a long high storeroom, empty except for a few scattered crates and boxes, and an old-fashioned roll-top desk in the far corner. Ian looked round. 'Well, there's nothing here.'

The Doctor agreed. 'I'm afraid the place has been abandoned for some time.'

There were shuttered windows on the far side of the room, and Ian threw them open. As the shutters creaked back, sunlight streamed into the dusty room. Ian looked out of the high window, his eyes widening at the panorama of ruined London before him. Below, the river flowed sluggishly through a desert of half-ruined buildings. 'Doctor,' he called. 'Come over here and look!'

The Doctor shook his head sadly at the view. 'Just as I feared. Some unimaginable catastrophe has over-taken London.'

Ian pointed to a square building just across the river. 'Look, there's Battersea Power Station,' he said dazedly. 'It's only got three chimneys. What's hap-pened to the other one?'

The Doctor waved at the surrounding desolation. 'What's happened to all London, my boy? That's the real question.'

The Doctor moved away from the window and be-gan hunting through the desk in search of clues. Sud-denly he said, 'Ah,' and triumphantly held up a grimy sheet of paper. 'Well, at least we know the century. This is the remains of a calendar.'

Ian ran across the room and almost snatched the paper from the Doctor's hand. It was a calendar right enough, the familiar pattern of numbered squares. Ian looked unbelievingly at the bold black figures at its head. They read '2164'.

He stared at the numbers, unable to take in what they meant. Slowly realisation dawned. He'd travelled two hundred years into 'his' future.

The Doctor put a consoling hand on his shoulder.

'I'm sorry, my boy, believe me. We must get back in the TARDIS and try again. I'll get you home.'

Ian nodded, unable to speak. The sounds from across the river came as a sudden distraction. 'What's that?'

The Doctor went over to the window. 'Gunfire! This city isn't quite dead after all.'

'Well, we'd better carry on searching. We may find *something* we can use.'

The Doctor slapped him on the back. 'That's the spirit, my boy.' They started searching the room, rooting through crates and boxes, most of which were empty or filled with useless junk.

The Doctor pulled aside an empty crate to get at the one behind—and a figure slumped to the floor at his feet. 'Chesterton! Over here,' he called.

Ian knelt to examine the body, which had fallen face-upwards. It was a middle-aged man, his body as grimy and neglected as his uniform. Clamped to his head was a strange helmet-like device, a gleaming metal affair fitting round the neck and over the head. Ian looked up. 'He's quite dead, Doctor. What's this metal thing for?'

The Doctor bent to take a closer look. 'Just what I was asking myself. Not for ornament, we can be sure of that.'

'Could it be some kind of surgical device—support for a fractured skull, or broken neck?'

'It's too complex for that,' said the Doctor thoughtfully. 'You know what I think, Chesterton—it's an extra ear, a device for picking up ultra high frequency radio waves.'

'A kind of communications system?'

'That—or some method of radio-control . . .'

Ian noticed a couple of objects thrust into the dead

man's belt. A truncheon—and a whip. He pulled out the whip, a vicious-looking device with a stubby black handle and long leather thongs, tipped with lead. He passed it over to the Doctor, who examined it with distaste. 'Worse and worse. Whoever this chap was, I'm glad we didn't run into him while he was still alive.'

'Any idea *what* killed him, Doctor?'

'He doesn't seem to be lying quite flat. If we turn the body over ...' They turned the body on its face. The black hilt of a knife was jutting out from under the left shoulder blade. 'Just as I thought,' said the Doctor grimly. 'He was murdered.'

From outside the room came the sound of a creaking floorboard.

Ian grabbed the truncheon from the dead man's belt and crept stealthily towards the door. He peered out into the corridor. It was empty. The Doctor close behind him, Ian crossed the corridor and pushed open the door of the room on the opposite side. 'Just another storeroom—and it's empty.' They went back into the corridor and Ian looked up and down it. 'The sounds were coming from somewhere out here.' He moved along the corridor and tried another door. It was locked. Ian rammed it with his shoulder, the door burst open, and he found himself shooting into empty space ... The Doctor quickly grabbed him by his coat and heaved backwards, and they both landed up in a heap in the corridor. Ian scrambled up and looked cautiously out of the door. Once it had led to a wooden staircase running down the outside of the building. But now the staircase was shattered and the door gave on to a sheer drop. Ian helped the Doctor to his feet. 'Well no one could have gone that way,' he said grimly.

The Doctor dusted himself down. 'Only someone

like you would even try,' he replied acidly. 'I suggest we abandon this fruitless search and return to the others.'

It was clear that the Doctor had had enough. Ian was inclined to agree with him. It wasn't very likely they'd find a full set of oxy-acetylene tools lying about waiting for them. And maybe hunting for the unseen killer wasn't such a brilliant idea either. 'All right, Doctor, come along.' Ian turned and led the way back downstairs.

They'd reached the warehouse door, and were about to step out into the open when the Doctor grabbed Ian's arm. 'Chesterton, *look*!' The Doctor's other hand was pointing upwards. Ian looked, and gave a gasp of sheer incredulity. Drifting low over the ruined buildings, for all the world like a plane coming in to land, was a flying saucer.

Instinctively Ian ducked back. The Doctor muttering, 'Fascinating, fascinating,' stepped out into the open to get a better look. Ian grabbed him and pulled him back into cover.

From the shelter of the doorway they watched the saucer drift slowly downwards. It looked exactly like the classic flying saucer of science-fiction films and drawings, silvery-coloured, oval in shape, and with rows of windows round the exterior. It made a low droning sound as it moved, disappearing behind some buildings.

Ian shook his head wonderingly. 'There were rumours of flying saucers in my time, Doctor. But I never thought I'd see one as close as this.'

The Doctor rubbed his hands together. 'Well, it settles one question. Whatever happened to London was not caused by the people of Earth. That was an interplanetary spaceship, my boy. Earth has been invaded by some other world.'

'Which explains the dead man we found,' said Ian thoughtfully. 'That thing on his head must have been some kind of alien control-device. And that gunfire we heard means somebody's still resisting the invaders.' Ian looked at the Doctor in sudden alarm. 'Barbara and Susan! We've got to find them and warn them what's going on.'

They ran back to the TARDIS at top speed. Barbara and Susan were nowhere to be found.

Ian looked angrily round the building site. 'Why will they do it?' he demanded. 'Why must they always go wandering off?'

'Perhaps they heard the gunfire from across the river,' suggested the Doctor. 'Or they might have seen the saucer, and run to hide.'

Ian sighed. 'Well, I suppose we'll just have to look for them.'

They searched the building site without success, then started working their way towards the river. At the top of the embankment steps they found their first clue ... a grubby, water-soaked handkerchief.

The Doctor nodded keenly, looking, thought Ian, like a rather elderly Sherlock Holmes. 'So far so good, Chesterton, my boy. They came here for water, something frightened them, and they ran off again.'

'Why didn't they run back to find us?'

The Doctor frowned at the interruption to his fine flow of deduction. 'I can't imagine,' he snapped. 'We shall just have to look further afield.'

They turned to leave—and found four uniformed men barring their way. They were ragged, gaunt, emaciated—and each one wore a shining metal device clamped to his head. They held truncheons in their hands.

Ian and the Doctor stood quite still. 'We won't get past them, Doctor,' Ian whispered.

'Then we must go down the steps.'

'Swim for it?'

'What else?'

Ian looked at the Doctor. For all his tetchiness, he was certainly a game old boy. 'All right. They don't seem to have guns. I'll try talking first.' Ian called out a hearty 'Hello!' At the same time he and the Doctor began edging their way down the steps.

The four men moved steadily after them. One was a little ahead of the rest. Suddenly he bellowed, 'Stop!' His voice was slurred and dragging, like a record played at the wrong speed. As he spoke he picked up a jagged chunk of masonry, and the other men did the same.

Ian and the Doctor continued their steady retreat. As they neared the water Ian whispered. 'When I give the word, turn and dive!'

'Ready when you are, my boy.'

'Right—now!'

They both turned, and froze in horror. A Dalek was rising from the water and advancing menacingly towards them.

3

The Freedom Fighters

When the flying saucer passed overhead, Barbara and Susan were already fleeing through the ruins of London with a man who called himself Tyler. He was a tough looking character, burly and middle aged, and although his manner was curt and brusque he didn't seem to be hostile.

When he'd grabbed Barbara at the steps, he'd released her almost at once, saying he'd just wanted to make sure she didn't scream. 'They' had their patrols everywhere, and he'd already carried Susan to shelter so she wouldn't be spotted.

He'd taken Barbara to Susan, who was laying under one of the arches of the bridge, confused and frightened. Lifting Susan in his arms, he'd bustled them both on their way, promising to take them to a safe hiding place, and come back later for their friends.

When the drone of the saucer filled the air, Tyler immediately flung Susan and himself to the ground. 'Get down,' he whispered fiercely. Barbara obeyed, though she couldn't resist raising her head to watch the gleaming shape of the saucer glide out of sight. Then Tyler was on his feet again, picking Susan up. Ignoring their questions, he said brusquely, 'We must keep moving, we can talk later. We shan't be safe till we get underground.'

Still carrying Susan, Tyler led the way to the broken entrance of what had once been an underground railway station. He started carrying Susan down the stairs, but she struggled till he had to put her down. 'Wait! What about my grandfather and our friend?'

Tyler shrugged. 'We'll do the best we can for them.'

Susan wasn't satisfied. 'That's not what you said before!'

Barbara joined in. 'You promised you'd get the others. We don't *want* to be separated.'

'There isn't time to argue,' said Tyler savagely. 'If we stay on the surface we'll all be killed, and then who'll help your friends? Now *come on*.' They moved on down the steps, Barbara and Tyler supporting Susan between them.

Tyler led the way along dusty silent corridors and on to the platform. Strange posters covered the walls, not the usual announcements of films and plays and exhibitions, but severe looking official notices in heavy black type. Barbara paused to read one.

PUBLIC WARNING. DO NOT DRINK RAINWATER. ALL WATER MUST BE BOILED BEFORE CONSUMPTION.

In smaller letters beneath were the words, 'Issued by the European Emergency Commission.'

Tyler reached out and pressed the letter 'O' in 'NOT'. Part of the wall slid back to reveal a tiny gap. A grim-looking young man appeared, rifle in hand. Tyler said, 'O.K. David, it's me.' David stood aside and Tyler helped Barbara and Susan through the gap. The door closed silently behind them.

They were in a small tiled ante-room, furnished with a few battered tables and chairs. Barbara guessed it had originally been accommodation for London Transport staff. Susan collapsed thankfully into a chair, rubbing her ankle.

The young man called David looked curiously at the

two girls. 'Hullo, then, what have you got here?' There was a faint Scots burr in his voice.

'Found 'em wandering about down by the river. Sitting targets.'

Barbara was annoyed by his scornful tone. 'We've only just got back to London. We didn't know there was any danger.'

Tyler looked incredulous. 'Didn't know? No, I suppose you couldn't have known or you wouldn't have acted so stupidly.'

'Now, *listen* ...' began Barbara angrily. 'You drag us here ...'

David held up his hand. 'All right, you two, let's not fight among ourselves. Time for introductions. You already know Jim Tyler. My name's David Campbell.'

His friendly smile transformed the grim young face, and Barbara couldn't help smiling back. 'I'm Barbara, and this is Susan.'

'I hope you can cook.'

Barbara gave him a surprised look. 'After a fashion.'

'Good. We're short of cooks down here ... and my cooking's terrible.'

He turned back to Tyler, his manner serious again. 'One of the Robomen jumped me in the warehouse. I had to deal with him. We'd better stop using the place for storage though.'

Tyler nodded. 'All right. Tell Dortmun.'

Susan had only been half-listening to this conversation, but the mention of a warehouse made her look up. 'Are you talking about the warehouse near that building site—beside the river?'

David nodded. 'That's right. Just opposite the old power station.'

Susan tried to get up, then sank down again, wincing from the pain in her ankle. 'Then you must have seen the Doctor and Ian—they went in there.'

'There *were* two men—but I hid from them. I thought they must be enemies——'

An inner door opened and a wheelchair shot through it, halting abruptly. In the chair sat a middle-aged man with a strong deeply-lined face. The upper part of his body was muscular and powerful, and he propelled the wheelchair along with big hands gripping the wheels. But his legs were wasted and shrunken, covered by an old army blanket. His voice was deep and commanding, with nothing of the invalid about it. 'Where the devil have you been, Tyler?'

Tyler was obviously used to the newcomer's abrupt manner, and his reply was equally spirited. 'I got delayed. Ran into these two. What are you doing up here? You're supposed to stay below in the operations room.'

'I'm just as active as anyone, and don't you forget it.'

Tyler grinned. 'All right, Dortmun, all right.' Somehow Susan sensed that despite the angry way they talked to each other, these two men were old and close friends.

Dortmun spun the wheelchair to face Barbara and Susan. 'Well, I suppose we can use two more pairs of hands,' he said gruffly.

David winked at Susan, as if telling her not to be too put off by Dortmun's abrupt manner. 'This is Susan. And this is Barbara—she says she can cook!'

'Good!' Dortmun glared at Susan. 'And what can you do?'

Susan grinned cheekily at him. 'Me? I can eat.'

For a moment Dortmun glared at her, then he gave a grim smile. 'Well mind you leave some for me. David, where do you think you're going?'

The young man was already at the door. 'These two have friends, two men, still on the surface. I know roughly where they'll be—I thought I'd go and bring them in.'

Dortmun considered for a moment—and Barbara and Susan held their breath. Then he nodded. 'All right. But take care—and don't be too long.'

As David passed by her chair, Susan whispered, 'Thank you. Be careful.'

'Don't worry, I'll see you later.'

As David left, Dortmun headed his wheelchair towards the inner door. 'Come along. We'd better get below.' He stopped as he saw Tyler and Barbara helping Susan to get up. 'What's the matter with her?'

Susan hobbled to her feet. 'I happen to have sprained my ankle,' she said sharply. 'Don't worry, I'll manage. I'm just as active as anyone.'

Dortmun gave an approving nod. Clearly he liked people to stand up to him. 'All right, let's get moving.'

He sped the wheelchair through the inner doors, and Tyler, Barbara and Susan followed him.

Ian and the Doctor watched horror struck as the Dalek rose slowly from the water and glided along the bank towards them. Instinctively they turned to run. But the nightmarish figures of the metal-helmeted men had moved down the steps to cut off their escape.

The Dalek spoke in the harsh, grating tones Ian remembered from Skaro.* 'Robomen! Why are these humans wandering freely in a forbidden zone?'

In his slurred, dragging voice the leader of the Robomen replied, 'No explanation.'

'Where is the Robopatrol for this section?'

'Not known.'

* See 'Doctor Who and the Daleks'

'You will take his place until he is found. The human beings will be taken to the landing area.'

'Daleks,' whispered Ian. 'What are they doing here on Earth?'

'Leave this to me, my boy.' The Doctor marched boldly up to the Dalek. 'I demand that you release us at once.'

'We do not release prisoners.'

'Indeed? And by what right do you take prisoners in the first place?'

'We are the masters of Earth.'

The Doctor snorted disdainfully. 'Not for long, I promise you.'

The Dalek was both astonished and enraged by this defiance. 'You will obey us or die!'

The threat only made the Doctor more indignant. 'Die? And who are you to condemn us to death? That settles it. Whatever you're up to, I shall pit myself against you and defeat you.' The Doctor folded his arms and glared defiantly at the Dalek. Ian closed his eyes and held his breath, mentally willing the Doctor to shut up. He was all in favour of opposing the Daleks, but he saw no use in getting themselves blasted on the spot.

The Doctor's words seemed to touch off one of those typical speeches, a mixture of threats and boasts, which seemed to be the Daleks' only form of communication with other species. 'We have heard many such speeches from the human leaders. All have been destroyed. Resistance is useless. It must cease immediately.'

'Oh must it? You surely don't expect the people of Earth to welcome you with open arms. Even Daleks can't be that stupid.'

'We have already conquered Earth.'

'Don't you pathetic creatures realise? You'll never

conquer Earth, not unless you destroy every living being——'

The Dalek's patience was clearly exhausted. 'Take them! Take them!' it screeched.

Robomen grabbed Ian and the Doctor by their arms and dragged them away. In their ears echoed the angry voice of the Dalek. 'We are the masters of Earth. We are the masters of Earth. We are the masters of Earth ...'

From his hiding place nearby, David Campbell watched helplessly as the Doctor and Ian were led away. He had arrived just in time to see their capture. There was little he could do to help them, not with Robomen present in such force. But at least he could find out where they were being taken. Slipping cautiously through the ruins, David began trailing the Robomen and their prisoners.

Survivors of London. The Daleks are the masters of Earth. Surrender now and you will live. Those wishing to surrender must stand in the middle of any street and obey the orders they will receive. Obey the Daleks!'

The radio went silent. Dortmun crashed his fist on the table, making the set jump and rattle. 'Obey motorised dustbins! We'll see about that! Tyler, come to the office, I want to talk to you.'

Barbara and Susan looked at each other. They were in a long underground room, filled with rows of trestle tables, at which people sat quietly working. Some were cleaning or assembling weapons, others were working on radio sets and a variety of technical equipment. One corner was sectioned off into a kind of canteen, where women and girls were preparing food, and in another

33

was the partitioned-off room into which Dortmun had just disappeared. Susan noticed that everyone in the room was tired and grim-faced. The place was obviously the main headquarters of the anti-Dalek resistance movement.

Tyler hesitated a moment before following Dortmun. He called, 'Jenny, come over here a moment, will you?'

A small dark girl got up from the nearest table and walked across to them. She stood before Tyler unsmiling, as if resenting the interruption to her work. 'Well?'

'Two newcomers. See if you can find them something to eat. One of them has a bad ankle.'

The girl looked unsmilingly at Susan and Barbara, no hint of welcome in her face. 'All right.'

Tyler turned to go. 'David will be back soon. I'm sure he'll have news of your friends. He might even have them with him.' He disappeared after Dortmun.

Jenny said briskly, 'Right, who's got the bad ankle?' Susan held out her foot. 'I have.'

Jenny knelt beside her chair and examined the ankle with skilful but ungentle fingers, ignoring Susan's groan of protest. She straightened up. 'Just a strain, no bones broken. Why haven't you put a cold compress on it?'

'Because I've only just got here,' said Susan spiritedly. She'd no intention of being bullied by someone no older than herself, and she'd taken an immediate dislike to this cold-faced and bossy girl.

Jenny turned to Barbara. 'I'll see to this ankle. You go over there and get some food. While you're at it, put your names down for a work detail.'

Protectively Barbara said, 'Susan won't be able to do much, not till her foot's better.'

34

'She can work sitting down, can't she? We've no room for useless mouths here.' Jenny moved away.

Barbara glared after her angrily. Like Susan, she didn't take kindly to being bossed about. But she reminded herself that they were dependent upon these people, not only for food and shelter, but for help in finding Ian and the Doctor. It wouldn't do to upset them—at least until Susan's ankle was better. Barbara gave Susan a rueful grin, and went meekly to fetch the food. From inside the little office came the noise of voices raised in anger. No one took any notice. It was only Dortmun and Tyler having another shouting-match. Everyone was used to that . . .

Dortmun slammed his fist on the desk. 'We must attack them, Tyler. We must attack now!'

'That's all very fine. But how? We've got about twenty able-bodied men and women, the rest are old folk, and kids.'

'Ample!' snapped Dortmun defiantly.

Tyler groaned. 'Ample? To attack the Daleks? Remember the wars in the twentieth century, Dortmun, when men with bayonets attacked machine-gun posts? They got mown down, defeated by superior technology. So would we be . . .'

'Don't lecture me, Tyler!'

'Then don't ask the impossible. You haven't been in the streets for quite some time. The Daleks have increased the Robopatrols, tightened up their security. It's almost suicide to go out there these days.'

Dortmun hammered the arm of his wheelchair. 'All right, I know. I'm in *this*! I send others, but I don't have to go myself!'

Tyler's tone softened. 'I didn't mean that and you know it. Now then, how's this new bomb of yours getting on?'

The distraction worked, just as Tyler had hoped. Eagerly Dortmun wheeled his chair to a table in the corner of the office, where shining glass spheres were set out on a blanket. 'All finished,' he said proudly.

'Have you tested it yet?'

'Tested it? It doesn't need testing, it's perfect. This is the bomb that will destroy the Daleks! Look, here's the casing, the new formula explosive, the detonating device ...' Eagerly Dortmun began to explain the workings of the bomb on which he had laboured so long.

He was still doing it when David Campbell slipped into the room some minutes later. David had seen Barbara and Susan as he came in, but they'd had their backs turned and he'd been able to slip into the office without their noticing him. Dortmun looked up. 'We're just discussing the next attack, David. How did you get on?'

'I brought back some more tinned food. There's quite a bit left in that department store.'

Tyler nodded. 'All right, I'll send out a foraging party. What about the two strangers?'

'Just as I got to the embankment I saw them being taken away. I followed them part of the way. Judging by the direction, they were taking them to Heliport Chelsea, where the Dalek saucer landed.'

Dortmun shrugged dismissively. 'Then that's the end of them. Once the Daleks get them inside that saucer, they're done for!'

David thought for a moment. Then he said, 'Not necessarily Dortmun. You listen to me ...'

4

Inside the Saucer

Guarded by Robomen, the Doctor and Ian were standing in what had once been the Chelsea Helicopter Port —Heliport for short. It was a wide stretch of open tarmac, surrounded by ruined buildings. Towering above them rose the immense gleaming shape of the Dalek spaceship. Together with a group of other prisoners, the Doctor and Ian were being held at the foot of a ramp which led up into the ship. Dalek patrols glided to and fro, guarding the perimeter of the Heliport.

Ian moved closer to the Doctor. 'Why are they keeping us waiting about here?' he whispered.

'I imagine this is an assembly point, my boy. They're going to take all their prisoners on board at once.' The Doctor nodded towards the other side of the Heliport. A group of Robomen were marching two more prisoners to join the main group.

Ian looked round at his fellow captives. They were grimy, ragged and defeated-looking. He turned back to the Doctor. 'I still don't understand all this. The Daleks were destroyed. We were there on Skaro, we saw it happen.'

Sadly the Doctor shook his head. 'The devastation may not have been as complete as we imagined. The Daleks have incredible tenacity, tremendous powers of survival. There may have been other colonies, on other parts of Skaro ...' He looked at the scene around them, the ruined city, the enormous spaceship, the blank-faced, helmeted Robomen standing guard over their prisoners. 'Anyway, however it happened, the Daleks have survived. And they've evolved too.'

Ian studied one of the Daleks as it glided past. 'I see what you mean. These do look a bit different. I wonder if that's got anything to do with their increased power of movement. On Skaro they could only travel in their own metal city.'

'Quite true. But this is an invasion force, remember. They've found ways to adapt themselves to new planets. Something on the hover-craft principle I should imagine.'

By now the two newcomers had been herded across to the main group. They were tough looking characters, one tall and wiry, the other short and thickset. Ian thought they looked less cowed than the other prisoners. A Dalek glided up to the Robomen guards accompanying them. 'Where are the other members of your patrol?'

In a slurred emotionless voice one of the Robomen answered, 'These men killed them both.'

Angrily the Dalek spun round, its gun-stick pointing at the prisoners. 'What are your names?'

'Bill Craddock,' said the taller man defiantly.

With equal truculence the thick-set man said, 'And I'm Mick Thomson. Want to put us in your hall of fame, do you?'

The Dalek's eye stalk swivelled towards them. 'Craddock and Thomson,' it repeated. 'You will be punished for your crimes. Robomen, continue your patrol.'

The Robomen moved away, and the Dalek addressed the group of prisoners. 'You will remain here without moving until it is time to enter the ship.'

Ian heard the man called Thomson mutter, 'We'll never escape once they get us inside there. I'm going to try something now, are you with me?'

Craddock glanced around. Daleks were on patrol everywhere, constantly moving round the edges of their group. 'Don't be a fool, man. You haven't got a chance.'

There was a note of hysteria in Thomson's voice. 'They're not getting me back in their filthy mine.'

A Dalek moved closer. 'The prisoners will be silent.'

Suddenly Thomson shoved Craddock to one side, dodged around the Dalek, and began tearing across the Heliport at full speed. Almost immediately a Dalek appeared to block his path. Thomson changed direction, wheeling to his left, but here too a Dalek was waiting. He dodged desperately to and fro, like a chess-pawn threatened by more powerful pieces, but the Daleks were ahead of him at every turn. At last a group of them encircled him—there was nowhere to run. Thomson called desperately to his friend. 'Craddock—help me!'

Instinctively Craddock took a step forward, but the Doctor held him back. 'Don't be a fool! There's nothing you can do. Our time will come.' Such was the confidence and authority in the Doctor's voice that Craddock found himself obeying without question.

They heard a grating Dalek voice. 'Kill him!' Several Daleks fired at once, and Thomson twisted and spun under the agonising impact of the Dalek death-ray. His body crumpled to the ground.

A Dalek moved menacingly back towards the horror-struck prisoners. 'Any further defiance will be punished in the same way. Prisoners will wait until it is time to enter the ship.'

In a corner of the main operations room, David was

breaking the news of the Doctor's capture to Susan. He glanced across to the other side of the room, where Barbara was helping to prepare a meal. 'I thought perhaps we wouldn't tell Barbara—not just yet anyway.'

'Oh, but I must,' protested Susan.

'Listen,' said David urgently. 'Dortmun's keen to make an immediate attack on the Daleks. He's got a new type of bomb he wants to test. Now, I managed to persuade him that the saucer would be a natural target. We can put off telling Barbara until the attack is over.'

Susan was beginning to understand what he meant. 'If the attack's a success, there's a chance that Ian and the Doctor will be rescued?'

David took her hand. 'Exactly. And if it isn't—well, they'll have just disappeared. At least there'll still be hope.'

They were interrupted by Jenny, who held out a batch of Roboman helmets to David. 'You wanted these?'

'Yes I did, thank you.'

'Well, here they are, take them. I've got more important things to do than wait on you.'

'You're a model of patience and charm, aren't you, Jenny?'

'I don't believe in wasting time.' Jenny glanced at David's hand, which was still holding Susan's. 'And I don't believe in sentiment, either.'

Her work finished, Barbara came over to them. She looked curiously at the pile of helmets. 'What's all this?'

'An invention of the Daleks,' said David grimly. 'We took them off dead human beings—human beings who'd been turned into Robomen.'

'There aren't that many Daleks on Earth,' explained Jenny, 'so they need helpers. They operate on some of their prisoners and turn them into sort of human robots, radio-controlled by these helmets. David's trying to find some way to block the Dalek transmissions that's why we're collecting these things.'

David picked up a helmet. 'The Daleks call the operation the Transfer. These helmets here transmit the Dalek orders direct to the human brain—at least for a time. Eventually the effectiveness of the operation wears off.'

Susan looked at the gleaming metal helmets and shuddered. 'What happens then? Do the people become human again?'

Jenny shook her head. 'The process burns out the circuits of the brain. In the end the Robomen go mad and die. They seem to get a sort of suicidal urge. They throw themselves off buildings, into the river ... That's why the Daleks need so many prisoners—to keep up their supply of Robomen.' David frowned warningly at Jenny, but she went on with her story. 'They take them to their flying saucer and operate on them. Once they've got you on board, there isn't a hope.'

Unaware of the shattering effect of her news on Susan, Jenny moved away. Susan looked at David. Perhaps it was just as well they hadn't told Barbara what had happened to the Doctor and Ian.

'*Move!*'

Obedient to the Dalek voice, the line of prisoners began shuffling up the ramp. The Doctor looked up at the Dalek ship as they moved inside. 'A work of genius, Chesterton.'

Ian was less enthusiastic. 'It's impressive enough. And it looks escape proof.' The interior of the Saucer was built in the Dalek style that Ian remembered from Skaro. Walls, doors, floors and ceilings were all of gleaming metal, everything utterly bleak and functional.

The Doctor rubbed his hands. 'Only on the surface, my friend. There's always a weak point—if you can find it.'

The Daleks were marching them along a curving metal corridor. The leading Dalek stopped, and touched a control. 'The first three prisoners will move into this cell.' The Doctor, Ian and the man named Craddock were the first three in line. The Dalek herded them into a cell and closed the door after them. 'Remaining prisoners—move!' Obediently the line of prisoners shuffled on.

In the control room, a Dalek stood watching the scanner screen. This Dalek was larger than the others, and its casing was a dull jet black. This was the Dalek Supreme, the Black Dalek, Commander of the expedition to Earth. On the scanner was a view of a prison cell, with the Doctor, Ian and Craddock sitting on the floor, their backs against the wall. The Dalek Supreme touched a control and the hidden camera zoomed in until the Doctor's face filled the screen. 'This is the one?'

Another Dalek replied. 'That is so, Commander. He defied us, spoke of resistance. His words betrayed superior intelligence and determination.'

The Dalek Supreme turned away. 'We shall await the results of the experiment.'

Unaware that he was the subject of a Dalek experiment, the Doctor was chatting to his fellow-prisoners, discussing the only subject of real interest—escape. 'I had a good look in that corridor outside. Plenty of scanners about.'

Craddock glanced round the cell. 'Can't see any in here. They may be hidden. What do you make of this thing, Doctor?' He pointed to a semi-transparent crystal box, packed with complex machinery, which was mounted on the wall near the cell door.

'I've a theory about that. I'll investigate it in a moment. Let's continue to survey the general situation.'

'I noticed what looked like a loading bay, Doctor,' Ian contributed. 'It should lead to the ground. There might be a guard outside, though.'

'There will be,' said Craddock gloomily.

'Our task is to escape,' said the Doctor sharply. 'You'll do no good sitting here moping.'

'And you'll do no good fooling yourself,' growled Craddock. 'Once the Daleks have got you, that's it!'

The Doctor shook his head reprovingly, and moved across to the crystal box. He began studying it closely. Ian said, 'How did all this start—the invasion of Earth, I mean?'

Craddock stared at him. 'Where've you been, on one of the moon stations?'

'Something like that,' replied Ian vaguely. 'I never got the full story.'

Craddock was silent for a moment, then he began to speak in a low, bitter voice. 'The meteorites came first. They bombarded Earth about ten years ago. A freak cosmic storm, the scientists said ... Then people started dying—some new kind of plague.'

'Germ warfare?' suggested Ian.

Craddock nodded. 'The Daleks were waiting, up there in space, waiting for Earth to get weaker. Whole continents were wiped out. Asia, Africa, America. Everywhere you went, the air smelled of death. The doctors tried all kinds of new drugs, but none of them worked. By now the world was split up into tiny struggling communities, too far apart to help each other. About six months after the plague had begun, the first of the flying saucers landed ...'

Ian listened in fascinated horror as Craddock went on with his story. The Daleks had flattened whole cities, striking ruthlessly at any sign of resistance. They had captured untold numbers of human beings, turning them into Robomen, discarding them when they died and creating new ones. Other human beings had simply been enslaved, made to toil in the Dalek mines under the whips of the Robomen.

The catalogue of horrors went on, until Ian could bear it no longer. *Why?* he interrupted. 'That's the one thing you haven't told us. Why are they doing all this? What has Earth got that they want so much?'

Craddock looked dully at him. 'I don't know, no one knows. But it's something under the ground. They've turned most of Bedfordshire into one gigantic mining area...'

The Doctor, who had been only half-listening, turned round impatiently. 'Never mind all this blab about Bedfordshire. I think I've discovered how this thing works.'

Ian went over to him. 'All right, Doctor. What is it?'

The Doctor pointed to a small metal rod clamped into a holder beside the box. Fixed next to it was a lens with a handle, looking like a pocket magnifying glass. 'Just hand me that, will you, my boy?'

'I wouldn't touch it,' warned Craddock.

Ian looked at the Doctor, who beamed infuriatingly at him. Carefully Ian took out the rod and handed it to the Doctor. 'There you are. Now what?'

'First, an experiment.' The Doctor moved the rod close to the transparent box. As if in sympathy, a similar but much larger metal rod *inside* the box began to move. 'You see, it's magnetic.'

'Marvellous,' said Craddock sarcastically. 'How does it help us?'

'And why's the box here at all?' asked Ian. 'What do the Daleks use it for?'

The Doctor nodded approvingly. 'An excellent question, my dear chap. Now, suppose you were a Dalek shut in here, how would you get out?'

Craddock frowned. 'Push up the door?'

The Doctor shook his head reproachfully. 'A Dalek has no hands, only a sucker. They rely on brain, not brawn.'

Ian looked at the crystal box, the lens and the metal rod. 'Are you telling me this set-up is some kind of key?'

'Precisely. All we have to do is open the box and use the key. Now then, pass me that lens, will you?'

Ian handed it over, examining the handle. 'You know I think you're right, Doctor. This thing is obviously made for a Dalek to hold.'

The Doctor gave him an encouraging smile. 'You're a good lad, Chesterton, you really do try hard. Now we must find the correct refractive index, or the box will probably explode.'

The Doctor began moving the lens about near the top of the box. Craddock watched him sceptically. 'Refractive rubbish,' he muttered. 'You don't think the Daleks would leave the key in here for us to find.'

'They have only contempt for human intellect,' said the Doctor sharply. 'And if all their prisoners are like you, I'm not so sure they're wrong ...' The Doctor started muttering abstruse calculations to himself. 'Did you ever do applied three dimensional graph geometry at your school, Chesterton?'

Ian shook his head. 'Only Boyle's Law.'

'Let's boil down this problem then, shall we?' Chuckling at his own excruciating pun, the Doctor added, 'Cover your eyes, gentlemen, this may be nasty.'

Craddock shook his head scornfully. 'I suppose it'll turn into a great big pumpkin or——' He broke off in astonishment. The lid of the crystal box had sprung silently open. 'Hey, it's a flaming miracle.'

Ian slapped the Doctor on the back. 'Doctor, sometimes you amaze me!'

'Only sometimes?' The Doctor chuckled. 'Now, all we've got to do is find the way to use this bar ... it'll be something to do with static electricity, I imagine. Now, if I push the bar in the box back with this one ...'

Craddock looked at the two bars. The one in the Doctor's hand was tiny, the one in the box large and heavy. 'You're going to push *that*—with *that*?'

'Exactly. And since similar poles repel, and both bars are magnetic ...'

The Doctor moved the small bar close to the large one. Immediately the large bar slid back—and the cell door moved smoothly upwards.

Craddock looked admiringly at the Doctor. 'You're a genius!'

The Doctor waved a deprecating hand. 'Oh it was nothing, nothing at all ... Now let's get out of this infernal flying machine and find Susan and Barbara.'

They ran out into the corridor and straight into a waiting group of Daleks and Robomen. The Black Dalek dominated the group. 'He has passed the escape test. Take him.' Robomen grabbed the Doctor and dragged him away. Others held back Ian as he tried to follow. He turned angrily to the Black Dalek. 'What are you going to do with him?'

The toneless Dalek voice replied, 'He will be robotised.'

5

Attack the Daleks!

The voice of the Dalek Supreme seemed to shake the little radio set. 'Rebels of London. This is your final warning. Leave your hiding places. Show yourself in the open streets. You will be fed and watered. Work is needed, but in return the Daleks offer you life. Continue to resist and we will destroy London. You will all die, the males, the females, the young of the species. Rebels of London, come out from your hiding places.'

The radio went silent. Dortmun gestured exultantly at the pile of shining glass grenades. 'We'll come out all right—with these. We don't need to hide any more, we can make *them* run.'

Barbara looked round the operations room, which was packed with grim-faced freedom fighters. Dortmun had called a meeting to listen first to the Dalek speech, and then to make one of his own. 'We'll answer their ultimatum for them—tonight. We're going to make a frontal attack on their flying saucer. Now *we* have the superior weaponry. One success and people will hope again. One victory will set this country alight. Then Europe, then the world. That's all we need—one victory!'

There was a roar of enthusiasm. Jenny's sceptical voice cut through it. 'How do we get within throwing range at the Heliport? The Daleks guard the perimeter —and they can fire long before we're near enough to use the bombs.'

Tyler didn't care for opposition. 'This will be a surprise attack, at night.'

Jenny wasn't convinced. 'The surprise will be over when the first bomb is thrown.'

Barbara jumped up. 'I've got it! You can use *these*.' She pointed to the pile of Robomen helmets at the back of the room. 'Some of the men can disguise themselves as Robomen. The rest can be prisoners they're bringing in. You'll be able to get right into the middle of the Heliport before they suspect!'

Tyler picked up one of the helmets and put it over his head. 'It'll work,' he said slowly.

Dortmun smiled grimly. 'Yes. It'll work. Let's prepare for the attack.'

Barbara, David and Susan crouched in a ruined house, overlooking the edge of the Heliport. The open area before them was brightly lit, the gleaming shape of the flying saucer towered above them. Patrolling Daleks moved silently around the perimeter.

All three were carrying satchels full of grenades. David tapped his meaningfully. 'Sure you've got it straight? As soon as Tyler and his attack group move in, we start chucking these.'

The two girls nodded. There was nothing to do now but wait. Susan rubbed her ankle, hoping it wouldn't let her down. Though still a little sore, it was almost better. She'd been determined not to be left out of the attack...

Inside the saucer the Doctor had been taken to a small room packed with intricate electronic machinery. Its central feature was a long table. Above one end was suspended an elaborate helmet-like device from which projected two metal prongs. For what seemed a very long time the Doctor was subjected to a variety of measuring devices which had recorded his blood-pressure, his temperature, the electrical activity of the brain, and indeed his total physical condition. The Robotising process was elaborate and time-consuming, and the Daleks did not care to waste it on subjects who might ruin everything by dying on them. At last the battery of tests was complete, and a Dalek scientist droned, 'Prisoner suitable subject for operation. Take him to the table.'

Two Robomen bustled the Doctor over to the table and stretched him out on it. Before he could move metal clamps were applied to hold him in place. His sleeve was pushed back and he felt a prick in his right arm. Immediately a numbing paralysis spread over his entire body.

The Doctor discovered he was unable to move a muscle. But although his body was immobilised, his brain was fully alert. Surely there was something he could do ... Surely something would turn up to save him. Or was this really the end, after all?

The Doctor lay quite still on the metal table. Dalek scientists glided around him, making final adjustments to the machinery that was designed to turn the Doctor into their helpless slave.

In the ruined house, David suddenly tensed. A dispirited-looking group of prisoners was being marched to the bottom of the saucer ramp, under the charge of a squad of Robomen. David drew a deep breath. 'Here they come. Get ready.' He took a grenade from his satchel, and prepared to throw.

Roboman helmet weighing heavy on his head, Tyler marched his squad of fake Robomen, with their equally fake prisoners, straight towards the ramp. The nearest Dalek guard moved up to him. 'Stop. What are you doing?'

Tyler made his reply in the slow dragging tones of the Robomen. 'I am taking the prisoners into the ship.'

'Wait. In which area were these prisoners captured?'

Tyler answered at random. 'Sector Four.'

'No patrol was ordered in Sector Four.'

Tyler did his best to bluff. 'New orders were given by the Dalek Supreme.'

Before the Dalek could reply there came the dull crump, crump, crump of exploding grenades from all around the Heliport. Barbara, Susan and David, and several other groups of freedom fighters, hurling grenades at random from widely different points, tried to create the impression of an attack from all sides. Forgetting Tyler, the Dalek guard began to scream, 'Attack warning. Attack warning!'

A siren started blaring from inside the ship. Daleks were rushing around in all directions. In his Roboman voice Tyler shouted, 'I will take the prisoners into the ship.' He marched his party quickly up the ramp.

Daleks were all round the perimeter of the Heliport now, firing in the direction of the explosions. But since the attackers were so few in number, and well spaced out, they were very hard to find.

A Dalek sped close to the building in which David and the girls were hiding, firing almost at random. David yelled, 'Get down!' and swept the two girls to the floor. The blast of a Dalek ray-gun sizzled through the open window and set fire to the wall above their heads. A man ran past the window then dropped screaming as the Dalek fired again. David struggled to his feet. 'Right, that's it. They must be inside by now. Time for us to pull back.' They ran from the blazing building and disappeared into the darkness.

Tyler and his men dashed along the metal corridors of the Dalek ship. 'Right,' called Tyler, 'spread out. Free as many prisoners as you can before you use the bombs.' One of the freedom fighters began blasting open the door of the cell which held Ian and Craddock.

The noise of battle came only faintly to the Robotising room, and the Dalek scientist continued his work undistracted. Suddenly a harsh voice blared from a hidden speaker. 'We are under attack. Report to main ramp. General alert. Report to main ramp.'

Obediently the Robomen and the Dalek scientists began filing from the room. The last Roboman was about to leave when a Dalek scientist stopped him. 'The prisoner is already prepared. You will remain and supervise the operation.' The Roboman touched a control. The Robotising machinery started to hum and throb with power. The pronged, helmet-like device began to descend, coming closer and closer to the Doctor's head. Just as the prongs seemed about to sink into his forehead Tyler dashed into the room, and wrenched the helmet device to one side. It blew up in a shower of sparks. The Roboman ran forward, there was a brief struggle, and he dropped with Tyler's knife between his ribs.

Another freedom fighter ran in. Tyler called, 'Baker! Help me get this man off the table.' They unfastened the clamps and lifted the Doctor clear. He slumped limply in their arms. Tyler made a quick attempt to bring him round and then gave up. 'No good, you'll have to carry him. See if you can get him clear.' Baker began dragging the Doctor from the table. A Dalek voice blared from the speaker. 'All reserve Robomen into action. Destroy the invaders!'

From a new hiding place behind a ruined wall, David, Susan and Barbara surveyed the scene. Fires were blazing all round the perimeter of the heliport. The Daleks had now abandoned the search for their elusive attackers and were retreating back to their ship. Barbara gripped David's arm. 'Tyler's going to be trapped inside the ship! Are those bombs of Dortmun's really any use against Daleks?'

Susan said, 'I didn't see the bombs stop any Daleks. But there's too much smoke to see what's going on.'

David said nothing. He too had his doubts about Dortmun's bombs.

Jenny came tearing towards them, pausing only to hurl a grenade at the Dalek ship. David seized on her arrival with relief. 'Jenny, take these two back to H.Q. I'm going to see if I can get Tyler out of that ship.'

As David ran off, Jenny said, 'I'm not playing nurse to you two. I'm going with David.' She looked scornfully at Barbara and Susan. 'I should have thought you'd have wanted to come too. After all, your two friends are in there.'

Barbara looked at her in astonishment, then turned to Susan. The look on Susan's face told her the whole story. 'You knew. You knew all along.'

Susan was shamefaced. 'We didn't want to worry you before——'

Barbara was already running towards the Dalek ship.

Susan followed, and caught her by the arm. 'Barbara, where are you going?'

'To help David find Ian and the Doctor. We've got to get them out of there.' Pulling free of Susan's grasp, Barbara ran off.

Susan turned to find Jenny looking at her. 'Well, are you coming?'

'I suppose so, though what good *we* can do . . .'

Jenny wasn't listening. 'We'll do no good if we don't try. Come on, this way.'

Jenny ran off and Susan, still hobbling a little, did her best to keep up with her.

By now Tyler and his men were already rushing down the ramp, bringing with them all the released prisoners they could find. Ian was somewhere near the back of the confused bunch of men.

At the foot of the ramp, the Daleks were waiting to meet them. They fired into the crowd at point blank range, and men screamed and dropped all around. Tyler shouted, 'The bombs. Use the bombs!' He pulled a grenade from his satchel and hurled it at the nearest Dalek. There was an explosion, a blaze of flame, and a cloud of smoke. Then, through the drifting smoke, Tyler saw the Dalek moving inexorably towards him, quite unharmed. Dortmun's bombs were a failure. Tyler yelled, 'Scatter all of you. Run! The bombs are no good!'

Freedom fighters and escaping prisoners began to run in all directions. Remorselessly the Daleks pursued, shooting them down. Since he'd been at the back of the escaping crowd, Ian was still on the ramp when the battle started. He got a grandstand view of the unequal struggle. He saw the useless bombs exploding all around, producing flame and smoke, but doing very little damage. Two freedom fighters tipped a Dalek on to its side by main force—only to be themselves blasted down by more Daleks. Suddenly, he saw a familiar face face appear out of the darkness. 'Barbara,' he yelled desperately. 'Barbara, get back!' Barbara saw him and waved then she disappeared, swept up by the milling crowd.

Ian jumped down from the ramp, just as the ramp itself began retracting with a hum of power. Two Daleks appeared round the curve of the Dalek ship, their gun sticks trained on Ian. The lifting of the ramp had left a small gap between the base of the ramp and the ship itself. Instinctively Ian flung himself into the gap—just as the ramp started to come down again, closing the opening and trapping Ian inside the Dalek ship. Gun-sticks blazing, Daleks poured down the ramp...

Barbara shielded her eyes from the smoke, dodged the blast of a Dalek gun-stick, and stumbled straight into Jenny. One glance at the disaster and chaos around them had convinced even Jenny that the attack was hopeless. She grabbed Barbara's arm and started dragging her away. 'Come on. We're getting out of here.'

Barbara pulled away from her. 'But Ian's there—I saw him on the ramp. And where's Susan?'

'We got separated. I think she's with David. They'll both have to take their chances. There's a way through the sewers. If you don't come now, you'll get killed.'

Without waiting for a reply, Jenny ran off. After a last agonised glance at the spaceship, Barbara ran after her.

In the control room of the Dalek ship, the Black Dalek watched the scene outside the saucer on a scanner. The screen showed a confused picture of blasting Daleks, exploding grenades, and falling freedom fighters. The area around the saucer was littered with the crumpled bodies of those who had failed to escape.

The Black Dalek transmitted orders to those outside. 'The enemy are retreating. Recapture as many prisoners as possible. Block all exits from the area. Find the enemy attackers and exterminate them.'

Tyler was ushering the last of the survivors down an open manhole cover, in an alley behind a burning building. 'Hurry,' he shouted. 'They'll be here soon.'

He was just about to duck down the manhole himself, when he heard pounding footsteps. He hesitated, then yelled, 'Come on, over here ... Quickly!'

A man tore round the corner of the building, hesitated for a moment then started running towards Tyler. Seconds later a Dalek appeared in pursuit. It fired immediately, and the man screamed once then dropped to the ground. Tyler disappeared down the manhole like a rat into its hole, pulling the cover over his head.

The Black Dalek turned away from the scanner screen. 'The attack has been defeated.'

His number two came forward eagerly. 'Many prisoners have been recaptured. Most of the attacking rebels have been killed or wounded. Only a very few are still at large.'

There was cold fury in the voice of the Black Dalek. 'Find them. Find all survivors and destroy them.

They must be exterminated!'

In a ghastly chorus, the surrounding Daleks took up their leader's chant. 'Exterminate them! Exterminate them! Exterminate them!'

6

The Fugitives

The freedom fighters' operations room was almost empty. Jenny was bathing a cut on Barbara's head with a wet cloth, while Dortmun looked on in gloomy silence. There was no one else. The rest must have been captured or killed, thought Barbara wearily. She looked up at Jenny. 'You're sure you didn't see what happened to Susan? She was with you the last time I saw her.'

Jenny's voice was gruff. 'I told you. She caught up with David—we were going to look for you. Then there were all those explosions, and I just lost sight of her.' Barbara sighed, and Jenny's voice softened at the sight of her unhappy face. 'Don't worry, she may still turn up. There, your head's fine now. Just a scratch.'

There came the sound of movement from the corridor outside. Barbara looked up hopefully—but it was Tyler who came into the room.

'Your bombs are useless, Dortmun.'

The man in the wheelchair looked up. 'How many were killed?'

'It was a massacre. We didn't stand a chance.'

'*How many?*'

Tyler sighed. 'I don't know. Almost all of them, I think. A few got away before the Daleks sealed the area, one or two got out through the sewers ...' He picked up a rucksack and started to fill it with supplies.

Barbara said dully, 'The Doctor and Ian were in that saucer. I *saw* Ian ... just for a moment ...' her voice faltered, then she regained control. 'What about the Doctor? Did you see any sign of *him*?

'There was an oldish man,' said Tyler slowly. 'We found him in the Robotiser Chamber. Baker got him clear of the ship, but after that . . .' He shrugged, then turned to Dortmun. 'We'll have to get out of London.'

'Why? The Daleks have never looked for us down here.'

'That was before we attacked their precious flying saucer. We've stirred them up now. They'll search every inch—*destroy* every inch.'

'But I *must* stay here. I need to work on my bomb.' He looked up at Tyler appealingly. 'It only needs a little more work, the principle is sound . . .'

'Forget your bomb. It's a waste of time.'

'It's the answer. It's the *only* answer . . .' There was a mad obsessive determination in Dortmun's voice.

'And who's going to use it for you?' asked Tyler. 'Me? These two girls here? Use your intelligence, man.'

Jenny joined in. 'Tyler's right. London will be too hot for us now.'

'If we could just stay a few days longer,' persisted Dortmun.

Tyler shook his head decisively. 'No. I'm going to see if I can find any more survivors, then I'm heading North.'

Barbara got to her feet. 'Can I come with you? If Ian and the Doctor did escape, we might find them . . .'

Tyler shouldered the rucksack. 'I'm sorry, but you'd slow me down. I've got to go alone. Good luck.'

Barbara called, 'If you do see any of my friends . . .' But Tyler had already gone.

Jenny said, 'We must get out of here too.'

Dortmun looked at them with sudden eagerness.

'There's the other H.Q. People will be gathering there —your friends too, maybe. I can go on working on my bomb—there's a laboratory there ...'

'Dortmun, *please*——' began Jenny.

Dortmun was beyond reason. 'That's it, we'll go to the Transport Museum.' He looked hopefully at them. 'It means crossing London, going over one of the bridges ...'

Barbara sighed. 'All right, we'll come with you.'

Dortmun spun his wheelchair, and headed for his office. 'I'll just get my things together. You'd better pack some supplies.'

Jenny moved closer to Barbara, and said in a low voice. 'We'd stand a lot more chance on our own.'

'Maybe. But he won't stand *any* chance without us. You needn't come—if you don't want to.'

Jenny hesitated, then shrugged. 'Might as well. Maybe Dortmun's right ... people might start collecting at the other H.Q.'

By the time they had loaded two more rucksacks, Dortmun came out of the office, a satchel slung over his shoulder. 'We'd better be moving. It's nearly light now.'

He headed his chair for the door. As she followed him, Barbara said, 'Do you really think my friends might end up at this Museum?'

Dortmun nodded vigorously. 'It's possible. Yes, it's distinctly possible.'

Possible, but not very probable, thought Barbara wearily. In her heart she feared she would never see her missing friends again.

The Black Dalek was addressing his aides. 'Orders from Dalek Supreme Command. Rebels must be totally crushed. An intensive search of London is to be made. If necessary, the city will be totally destroyed.'

'Do you intend to remain in the city?' asked the second-in-command.

'No. The ship will now take me to the mine workings in the Central Zone.'

'We have recaptured many escaped prisoners.'

'They will be put to work in the mine. Feed and water them. They must be strong in order to work.'

'I obey.'

The second-in-command began issuing orders into a communications network. Dalek and Robomen patrols would cover all central London, seeking out and destroying rebel hiding places.

The Black Dalek swivelled to face the spaceship's flight operators. 'Prepare ship for lift-off!'

Although the Daleks didn't know it, there was at least one escaped prisoner who was still free, and still on the ship. After his dive into the hatch below the ramp, Ian had found himself in a service tunnel somewhere in the bowels of the ship. Wriggling between humming and throbbing Dalek machinery, he had gradually worked his way back to the upper levels. Immediately he headed for the Robotiser room, in the hope of finding the Doctor.

He slipped inside, glancing with a shudder at the central table and sinister electronic apparatus suspended above it. The place was completely empty, no Doctor, no Daleks.

He heard movement in the corridor outside and ducked behind a bank of instruments. Two men came into the room. One was slight and wiry, with curly black hair. Behind the first man, holding him in a painful armlock, was a tall figure that Ian recognised immediately.

He stepped from his hiding place. 'Craddock!'

Releasing his prisoner, Craddock swung round. His face was expressionless, and there was a gleaming metal device on his head. His voice was slurred and dragging. 'You are to be Robotised.'

Ian backed away. 'Craddock—it's me ...'

Craddock lurched forward and grabbed Ian's arm, trying to bend it behind his back. Ian struggled desperately. Although his movements were slow and clumsy, the Robotised Craddock seemed abnormally strong, and quite impervious to pain. A savage blow to his ribs produced only a grunt, and there was no slackening in the steady pressure on Ian's arm.

Ian decided to use skill rather than strength. Grabbing Craddock by sleeve and coat, Ian twisted round, bent and sent his opponent hurling over his shoulder in a judo throw. Craddock crashed to the floor, with enough force to stun any normal man. But Craddock was no longer normal. He scrambled immediately to his feet and advanced on Ian, hands outstretched. Despairingly Ian realised he was fighting not a man but a machine—a machine that couldn't be hurt, would never get tired and never give up ...

As Craddock's hands closed on Ian's throat, the wiry man joined in the struggle. He threw himself on Craddock, gripped the helmet-device with both hands, and ripped it from Craddock's head. The results were immediate and dramatic. Craddock let out a series of terrifying screams, his hands clutching his head. His body flopped to the floor and thrashed frantically like a stranded fish. His back arched in a final convulsion and he went limp and still.

Ian got up slowly, rubbing his throat. He examined

Craddock's body. As he'd expected, the man was quite dead. He looked at the wiry man and held out his hand. 'Thank's for the help—my name's Ian.'

The other returned the handshake. 'Larry. And thank *you*. I was on my way to ending up like *him*.' He nodded towards the body on the floor. 'He caught me hiding in one of the storerooms. I smuggled myself on board quite a while ago.'

'You did *what*?'

'This saucer makes periodic trips to the mine workings in Bedfordshire. My brother's one of the slaves there. I'm going to find him and get him out.'

'So you're hitching a lift with the Daleks? You don't choose the safest way to travel, do you?'

Larry grinned. 'Maybe not. But it's the quickest. What about you? What are you doing here?'

Quickly Ian explained how he'd been captured by the Daleks, freed during the raid, and trapped in the ramp housing straight afterwards. 'I'm looking for the friend who was captured with me,' he finished. 'Though I'm not even sure if he's still on board. There's a chance he got away during the raid.'

Larry started dragging Craddock's body towards the wall. 'We'd better put this down the disposal chute. They'll start hunting for us if it's found in here.'

Ian helped Larry to drag the body to a hatch set in the far corner. Larry slid back the hatch-cover, and immediately they felt a powerful suction dragging them towards the opening.

Between them they wrestled the body into the hatchway. Immediately the force of the suction snatched it down into the chute. Larry slid the cover back into place. 'Right, we'd better get out of here and find somewhere safer to hide.'

Suddenly there was a hum of power, and a steady

vibration all around them. Ian put a hand on the wall to steady himself. 'Looks as if you might get your trip to Bedfordshire after all. I think we're taking off!'

In the Control Room, the Black Dalek ordered, 'Maximum repulsion. Set course for mine workings in Central Zone.'

The Dalek spacecraft lifted slowly from the Heliport, which was still littered with the bodies of those who had died in the attack. It rose smoothly into the air and began skimming northwards over London, just as dawn was breaking.

From their hiding place, Susan and David watched the saucer disappear from sight. Susan wondered if the Doctor and Ian were still on board, or if they'd managed to get away during the raid. She had only a confused and nightmarish memory of her own escape. Daleks firing into the crowd of freedom fighters and escaping prisoners, the screams of the dying, the roar of explosions, sheets of flame and clouds of smoke. Somewhere in all the confusion David had grabbed her hand and pulled her clear. They'd escaped from the area just before the Daleks sealed it off, and they'd been stumbling through the ruins ever since. At last they'd arrived in the cellar of a ruined house, and here they'd stopped to rest. David explained it was one of the freedom fighters' regular hiding places. Although the house above it was in ruins, the cellar itself was warm and dry. It was furnished with battered old beds and chairs, and there were even stores of food, water, weapons and ammunition. A flight of steps led up from the cellar into an alleyway between rows of ruined houses.

From the cellar doorway, Susan saw the flying saucer disappear over the rooftops. 'Does that mean the Daleks have gone?'

David shook his head wearily. 'The saucer comes and goes regularly, ferrying prisoners to the mines. There are still plenty of Daleks and Robomen on the ground.' Suddenly he broke off. 'Get down—there's a patrol coming.'

They ducked back inside the cellar. Despite David's warning Susan couldn't resist peeping round the door. Two Daleks were gliding along the alleyway above them. Alert and suspicious, their eye-stalks swivelled to and fro, scanning all around them. Susan shrunk back inside the cellar, closing her eyes. After a moment, David touched her gently on the shoulder. 'It's all right —they've gone. We'll give them time to get well clear and then move on.'

'Move on where?'

'We'll have to try to get out of London, join up with one of the other groups.'

From the alleyway came the sound of pounding foot-steps. A Dalek voice grated, 'Stop! Surrender or you will be exterminated!'

The footsteps faltered then ran on. There was a scream of 'No ... no ...' and the crackle of a Dalek gun-stick. Then silence.

Susan shuddered and threw herself into David's arms. 'Why did we ever come here,' she said hysteri-cally. 'Why, why? If only we could get back in the TARDIS and just go away ... I'm sure the Doctor would let you come with us ...'

David said sadly, 'You get away if you can. But I can't.'

'Why not?'

'This is my world. My Earth. I can't just leave it,

clear off somewhere else.'

Susan looked at him wonderingly. 'I've never felt like that about anywhere. I left my own planet when I was very young, and we've been travelling ever since. I've never really *belonged* anywhere.'

David looked seriously at her. 'Someday you ought to stop travelling and really *arrive* somewhere—get down, someone's coming.'

'Daleks?'

'Don't think so. Human footsteps. Could be Robomen...'

Pushing Susan down into cover, David crouched in readiness at the bottom of the stairs. He slipped something from his belt, and Susan saw light glinting on the blade of a knife.

They waited as the dragging footsteps came closer...

7

Reunion with the Doctor

Susan cowered back as a monstrous, deformed shape appeared at the top of the steps. The huge misshapen figure began to descend the stairs ... As it came nearer, Susan realised she was looking not at one man but *two*, one carrying the other on his shoulders. And the man being carried was the Doctor!

Joyfully she ran forward calling, 'Doctor, it's me, Susan!'

David meanwhile had recognised the other man. He put his knife away, and helped the newcomer to lower the Doctor's body to the ground. 'Baker! Are you all right?'

Baker grunted with relief as he lowered the Doctor's body. 'I'm O.K. Worried about him, though.'

The Doctor was very still. His eyes were wide open but he seemed unable to move or talk. Susan looked anxiously at Baker. 'What is it? What's the matter with him?'

'Daleks drugged him. Should be beginning to wear off by now.'

The Doctor stared up at them. Slowly, very slowly, his lips moved and he said, 'Susan ...' Susan hugged him in happy relief.

Shrugging aside Susan's thanks, Baker told them of the disastrous aftermath of the attack, of how he'd managed to get the Doctor away early on. 'We were lucky. I think most of the others were killed or captured.'

'What will you do now?' asked David. 'Do you want to join up with us?'

Baker, a burly, taciturn character, was clearly something of a loner. 'No, the bigger the group, the bigger the risk. I'll make for the Cornish coast. Not so many Daleks down there.'

David handed over a flask and a packet of food. 'Here, take these. You'll need them.'

'What about you?'

'We'll manage. Plenty of food stored here—and not many left alive to eat it.'

Baker took the supplies and made for the cellar door. 'Thanks. I'm off then. Good luck.' He disappeared up the stairs, and they heard his footsteps moving along the cobbles of the alleyway.

Suddenly a metallic voice shouted, 'Halt!'

David ran to the top of the steps and peered out. He could see Baker halfway down the alley. A Dalek had appeared at the other end. Baker spun round. A second Dalek was blocking the alleyway behind him.

As both Daleks advanced towards him, Baker dropped his rifle and raised his hands. The second Dalek screeched, 'Exterminate!' Both Daleks fired at once. Caught in the double blast, Baker twisted in mid-air and died immediately. His body dropped to the ground. For a long moment the two Daleks scanned the alley with their eye-stalks. Then they glided silently on their way.

Shaken, David crept back to Susan. 'The Daleks just shot him down, wouldn't even let him surrender. They must have decided to kill everyone on sight.'

Susan was cradling the Doctor in her arms, getting him to drink a little water. 'Where can we go, David? What can we do?'

'Dortmun set up a second Command H.Q.—in the

68

old Transport Museum. If your friends have survived, that's probably where they'll make for. There are more supplies there too, bombs and weapons. Dortmun had quite a laboratory ...'

The Doctor groaned and started to sit up, and Susan helped him into a chair. 'How are you feeling now?'

The Doctor spoke with surprising clarity. 'The Daleks paralysed my body and my willpower, but not my mind. Really a most interesting experience.' He flexed his legs and found he could move them a little. 'It's wearing off, though. Wearing off fast.'

Susan hugged him again. 'You just have a good rest. As soon as you feel better, we're going to go and find Barbara.'

For Barbara and Jenny, the long journey across London was fraught with danger. Although it was now broad daylight, the fact that Dortmun was in a wheelchair meant they had to keep to roads and paths in fairly good repair, and prevented them from using the safe routes across the rubble and through the sewers. Time and time again they had to shove the chair into some doorway for cover, and crouch motionless while a patrol of Daleks glided by.

Most dangerous of all was crossing the river. They had decided to use Westminster Bridge, since that part of Central London seemed fairly free of Daleks. They had almost reached the bridge itself when Jenny called, 'Look out!' and they rushed into a shop doorway for cover. Barbara never forgot the sight that met her eyes when she peeped out. A patrol of Daleks gliding over Westminster Bridge, their sinister shapes profiled against the ornately decorated façade of the Houses of Parliament. It made an unforgettably symbolic picture. The squat metallic shapes of the alien invaders stood out against the building that represented so many centuries of human progress and tradition—a tradition the Daleks had ended with brutal abruptness. They watched in silence as the Daleks filed over the bridge and disappeared.

Dortmun nodded satisfied. 'There shouldn't be another patrol for a while. Come on, let's try to get across while we can.'

They pushed the wheelchair across the bridge and through the deserted streets of Belgravia without running into any more Daleks. The Civic Transport Museum was housed in an elegant exhibition hall, in a quiet side street.

Dortmun led them to a back entrance in a mews, and produced a key that opened a locked side-door.

They found themselves in a shadowy darkened hall, rather like a huge bus garage. All around stood vehicles of various kinds, roped off with explanatory placards nearby. There were milk-floats, taxis, old-fashioned open-topped buses, dust-carts—all the many kinds of vehicles that are part of the life of a big city. Some of the vehicles had still been in use in Barbara's day, and she wondered what had replaced them in this future age. Had Londoners *ever* solved their traffic problem? If they hadn't, thought Barbara, remembering the empty streets, the Daleks had certainly dealt with it for them.

At the back of the hall were various rooms intended for museum staff, including a workshop where Dortmun had established his laboratory. He made for it immediately, forgetting the two girls in his anxiety to get back to work on his one obsession—the creation of a bomb that would destroy the Daleks. Jenny disappeared too, scouting the area for signs of the enemy.

Several hours later, Barbara was prosaically employed in boiling a kettle in one corner of the hall. Behind a small screen she'd found a tiny kitchen alcove. There was a table and a gas-ring, a packet of tea in one of the cupboards, and an unopened tin of milk. The logical thing to do seemed to make a cup of tea. The typically English response to any crisis, thought Barbara with a smile as she poured water into a chipped china teapot.

A side-door flew open and Dortmun propelled himself towards her. The satchel over his shoulder was once more filled with gleaming grenades. 'It's finished,' he announced triumphantly. 'I've boosted the explosive charge. The problem is to crack the Daleks' outer casing. It's made from a metal called Dalekenium.'

Barbara looked doubtfully at the grenades. Would they really work this time? Dortmun had been just as confident before the disastrous raid on the Dalek flying saucer. She passed him a cup of tea. 'This Dalekenium ... could that be what they're mining for in Bedfordshire?'

'I doubt it. I imagine they mine Dalekenium on their own planet.'

'Then what are they looking for? Oil maybe? Some other metal?'

Dortmun shook his head. 'They could have picked on a hundred planets to find those things. But they're after something ... Something buried deep in the heart of Earth.'

Footsteps echoed through the great hall as Jenny came towards them. 'I've checked over the whole building,' she announced. 'Not a sign of anyone. But I think the Dalek patrols *have* been here—and I *know* some of our people have.'

Barbara poured her some tea. 'How can you be so sure?'

Jenny pointed to a mysterious symbol scrawled on a wall nearby. 'That's one of our message-signs. It means some of our people have been here and moved off towards the South Coast. Don't blame them either. London seems to be swarming with Daleks.'

Dortmun frowned. 'You think they've landed another force in London?'

'You saw for yourself. We were lucky to make it here through the streets. If things go on building up, we haven't a chance. We'll have to move on.'

Barbara's heart sank at the thought of another pointless, dangerous journey. 'Where can we go? What's the good of just running all the time?'

Jenny looked coldly at her. 'We're surviving, aren't we? That's what counts.'

Dortmun patted his satchel of grenades. 'We'll all survive. Now I've got this new-formula explosive ...'

Barbara looked despairingly at her two companions. Dortmun obsessed with perfecting the bomb that had become his reason for living, Jenny thinking only of running and hiding like some hunted animal. They needed someone who could look at the problem with a wider perspective. Barbara spoke her thoughts aloud. 'I wish the Doctor were here.'

Jenny looked surprised. 'He's just an old man, isn't he? What could he do?'

'He happens to be a brilliant scientist. He could *think*—which is more than the rest of you seem to be doing!'

'A scientist, you say?' Dortmun was immediately interested. 'I'd like to discuss my work with another scientist. If only we knew where he was ...'

'I've been thinking about that, trying to put myself

in his place. I'm sure he'd be intrigued by those mines in Bedfordshire. He'd want to take a look at them.'

Jenny said brutally, 'If he's still alive.'

'Of course he's still alive,' said Barbara angrily.

'Why? What's so special about your Doctor? He doesn't wear some invisible shield, does he?'

Dortmun spoke with sudden authority. 'Jenny! Go and take another look around.' As Jenny moved sulkily away, Dortmun said apologetically, 'She's not really callous, you know. She's been fighting the Daleks for most of her life.' Barbara nodded understandingly and he went on. 'I'd like you to try to find your friend the Doctor and give him this—it's the notes for my bomb.' He handed her a tightly folded bunch of papers, scrawled over with notes and incomprehensible diagrams...

Barbara looked at the papers in astonishment. 'Why can't you give them to him yourself?'

'I can, I can ... if we ever meet. But meanwhile I'd like you to take care of them. I'm not exactly mobile like this, am I? If something happened, I'd like my work to go on.'

For all his bitterness, thought Barbara, no one could deny Dortmun's courage. Crippled, defeated, hunted, his one thought was to go on fighting. She took the papers and laid them on the table. 'All right, I'll look after them if you like. But I'm not leaving you ...'

Dortmun gave one of his rare smiles. 'Thanks. Now then, if you'll round up Jenny, we can set out for those mines...'

Barbara didn't have to go far to look for Jenny. There were stairs on the other side of the hall, and Jenny came running down them, her footsteps echoing. 'Daleks! I saw them from an upper window. They're all over the place.'

Jenny's voice rang out across the hall. Nearby, Dortmun heard it, and came to a sudden decision. Clutching the bombs on his lap, he wheeled his chair towards the main doors.

Barbara and Jenny missed him as they ran down the other side of the hall. Barbara stopped in astonishment when she saw Dortmun wasn't where they'd left him. Jenny looked round. 'Where is he? He can't have gone outside, he wouldn't be so stupid.'

Barbara saw the papers on the table. 'Look, he's left the plans—but he's taken the bombs. I think he's gone to try them out!'

There was an echoing crash from the front of the hall. Daylight streamed in as the main doors were flung open. They turned and saw Dortmun in the doorway, heard his voice raised in defiant challenge.

'Daleks! Where are you, Daleks?'

The group of Daleks outside the museum's main door seemed frozen in astonishment as Dortmun appeared in the doorway. To be defied and attacked was a new experience for them, and they hesitated, fearing some trap.

Dortmun wheeled himself forwards straight at the nearest Dalek. When he was close enough he hurled the entire satchel of grenades. There was a shattering explosion, and a sheet of flame. A corner of the building collapsed, and Dortmun and his Dalek enemy disappeared beneath the rubble. Daleks milled about in confusion, shouting 'Emergency! We are being attacked!'

Picking up Dortmun's papers, Barbara pulled Jenny back into the shadows. 'They'll be here any minute. We've got to hide!'

Daleks moved cautiously into the hall, eye-stalks scanning the exhibits on either side. One of them trained its gun-stick on the waxwork of a milkman, posed stiffly beside his float. 'Halt! Who are you?' The waxwork, naturally enough, didn't move. Another Dalek examined it more closely. 'It is a sub-cultural effigy. Proceed with the search.'

Methodically the Daleks continued to search the hall. Barbara and Jenny retreated before them, dodging from one antiquated vehicle to another. Despairingly, Barbara realised they were being driven into a corner. The Daleks moved closer and closer, tightening the circle around the two girls ...

The Doctor was staggering determinedly to and fro across the little cellar, working off the remaining effects of the Dalek drugs. His face was grim and set as he fought to ignore the shooting cramp-like pains in arms and legs. Susan watched him in concern, realising the Doctor was quite likely to go on till he dropped. She caught him by one arm, and gently led him to a chair. 'Easy does it. That's enough for a first try.'

Thankfully the Doctor stretched his aching limbs. 'I never realised walking could be so exhausting. The numbness is most certainly wearing off though. I shall be able to travel in a short while.'

'Good. David says we should move North, join up with the resistance groups there.'

Susan saw at once that she'd made a mistake. The Doctor frowned and said sharply, 'My dear child, I don't care what that young man says. I make the decisions, and I think it best that we return at once to the TARDIS.'

'But we can't even get inside. David says London's swarming with Daleks. We'd never even get there alive.'

The autocratic side of the Doctor's nature came to the fore. 'Are you questioning my authority, child?'

'No, but David says ...'

'David says, David says,' mimicked the Doctor savagely. 'You seem to trust this young man's judgement more than you do mine!'

With a shock Susan realised the Doctor was quite right. Somehow she *had* grown to rely on David, to trust his judgement in every crisis. She felt safe when they were together. That was why she didn't want to leave him. Perhaps there were other reasons too ...

Returning from his scouting expedition, David heard raised voices, and listened to the last stages of the argument. He paused at the head of the cellar steps, realising he would have to move carefully. He was getting very fond of Susan, and he didn't want them to be separated. He ran down the steps into the cellar. The Doctor and Susan were glaring at each other, and scarcely seemed to notice him. David ignored the tension in the atmosphere. 'I didn't even get as far as the river. There are patrols everywhere. We'll never make it to the Museum.'

The Doctor snorted. 'I take it you're saying it would be impossibly dangerous to go back to the river too?'

David nodded. 'I'm afraid so. There are Daleks in this area of course, but not nearly so many.' He grinned reassuringly at Susan and turned back to the Doctor. 'I wanted to ask you—what would you suggest as our next move?'

The Doctor sat bolt upright. 'Me? Why do you ask me?'

'You're the senior member of the party, sir. Naturally, I'd like the benefit of your superior experience.'

The Doctor beamed. Clearly this young fellow David was a sensible chap after all. He considered carefully.

'Well, if you really want my advice ... I think we should head North, join up with some of the resistance groups there. I'm very keen to see what the Daleks are up to in this mine of theirs!'

Susan flung her arms round the Doctor and hugged him. 'Grandfather! Oh, Grandfather!' The Doctor returned her hug, winking at David over her shoulder. 'My dear child, what *is* all the fuss about?'

The Commander of the Dalek ground forces glided into the control room of the London base. 'Message from Dalek Supreme, now *en route* for mining area. Report on the destruction of rebel hiding places.'

The Dalek engineer gestured with his sucker towards an illuminated wall-chart. 'Destruction is proceeding. Rebel hiding places in areas one to three destroyed. Areas four to eight now in flames. Proceeding to lay charges in vicinity of suspected rebel hideout in area nine.' The sucker indicated a spot on the map ...

Two Daleks glided along the alleyway outside the basement in which the Doctor and his friends were hiding. Between them they pushed a small trolley on which stood a large metal canister. Dials and switches were set into the canister lid. One of the Daleks touched a control, and the canister began emitting a steady electronic bleep.

Leaving the trolley just at the head of the stairs, the Daleks turned and glided away. From somewhere in the distance there came the noise of an explosion.

Susan looked up at the sound of the distant rumble. 'What was that?'

'The latest Dalek tactic,' said David grimly. 'Block-buster bombs. They destroy whole sections of the city at a time. Anywhere the Daleks think we've a hideout, they just blow up the entire area.'

The Doctor was on his feet. 'Shouldn't we be on our way, my boy? If they suspect you've a hideout in *this* area ... ?'

Susan shivered. 'Must we? I don't like the sound of those explosions—and there may still be Daleks about.'

David put an arm round her shoulders. 'All right, we'll hang on a little longer. But the Doctor's right, we must go soon.'

A needle flickered on the detonation dial of the canister outside. The electronic bleep quickened as countdown entered the final phase ...

8

The Mine of the Daleks

Suddenly the Doctor held up his hand. Susan stared at him. 'What's the matter?'

'Listen!'

In the silence the electronic bleep sounded clearly. It was speeding up, and getting louder. The Doctor and his companions ran out of the basement. They stopped in horror at the sight of the gleaming metal canister at the top of the steps. 'What is it?' whispered Susan.

David's face was grim. 'One of the Dalek blockbuster bombs.'

Susan tugged at his arm. 'Quick, let's get clear ... run!'

David didn't move. 'No use. That thing's due to go off any moment. There's no way we could get out clear of the range of the blast.' He stood staring at the bomb as if paralysed by horror.

'In that case we'd better dismantle the thing,' said the Doctor briskly. He ran nimbly up the steps and leaned over the canister, studying the controls set into its top. 'Now then, this dial with the needle is the time mechanism. The red area at twelve o'clock signifies the detonation point, I imagine.'

David looked over his shoulder. 'So when the needle reaches the red, that will be it?'

The Doctor nodded. 'Help me prise the front off this thing, will you, my boy? I must destroy the timing control.'

David produced his knife and thrust it into the join between the main body of the canister and its lid. He heaved with all his strength—and the knife blade broke in two.

'I need some kind of a lever,' snapped the Doctor. 'Look around, both of you. A nail, a piece of metal, anything will do.'

Obediently David and Susan began searching the rubble. The Doctor went on working with the broken blade but without much success. The stub of the blade was too thick to go in the crack. He tossed it aside. Susan found a twisted piece of iron. 'How about this, Doctor?'

'Too big. There must be *some* way we can get in ... some tool.'

Suddenly David said, 'Acid! Those bombs of Dortmun's—the detonation mechanism is acid-based. Maybe we could burn through the casing.'

The Doctor nodded eagerly. 'It's a chance. Let's have one of them here. Quickly now!' David ran down into the cellar, reappearing almost immediately with his bomb-satchel. He ran back up the steps and handed the Doctor one of the fragile glass spheres.

The Doctor took it from him, and held it carefully on the top of the canister, just over the point where he estimated the timing mechanism to be. 'Pass me your piece of iron, Susan. Now, *if* I can manage to release the acid without detonating this bomb ...' Using the iron as a hammer, the Doctor gave the sphere a carefully measured tap, like a man cracking a boiled egg with a spoon. A crack appeared in the sphere and a colourless liquid started to trickle out. As it ran over the lid of the canister it *smoked*.

'Look,' whispered Susan. 'It's starting to burn through...'

A patch of the metal was beginning to crack and

crumble. The Doctor jabbed cautiously with the piece of iron, and the metal flaked and crumbled away. 'Splendid! Now your knife again, young man.' Feeling like the assistant surgeon at an operation, David passed the Doctor the broken knife.

The Doctor glanced at the detonation dial. The needle was now only a fractional distance from the red zone, and the bleep was rising even higher. But the Doctor's face was calm and his hand steady as he jabbed at the delicate mechanism with the improvised tool.

'Now, if I remove the fuse...' Carefully he lifted out a small section of the bomb's 'works'...

Suddenly the bleeping stopped. The needle on the detonation dial became still, and the Doctor leaned on the canister for support as he drew a deep gasping breath...

The Daleks finished their search of the Transport Museum and assembled outside. 'There are no more rebels in the building,' announced the patrol leader in confident tones. 'We shall continue the search elsewhere.'

The Dalek patrol moved away, leaving behind them a pile of rubble which entombed one of their number and the rebel leader Dortmun.

Inside the museum, Barbara and Jenny crept from the vintage corporation dustcart in which they'd been hiding. Although it was an unglamorous hiding place it had proved quite effective. The Daleks had searched all round the parked vehicles, but hadn't bothered to look inside any of them, perhaps not understanding the purpose of these alien machines.

Barbara peered out of the still-open front door. 'They've gone. But there's no saying they won't be coming back. We've got to get away from here.'

'How? With Dalek patrols everywhere, we'd be shot down as soon as we set foot in the streets.'

'Then we won't set foot.' Barbara waved her hand. 'With transport all around us, why should we have to walk?'

Ignoring Jenny's protests that the whole scheme was crazy and would never work, Barbara started checking over the vehicles in the hall. Some were too clumsy and antiquated, others too slow, and she settled at last on the sturdy corporation dustcart in which they'd hidden.

A search of the garage attached to the Museum produced tools, a foot-pump, and best of all, half a dozen cans of petrol under a tarpaulin. Soon Jenny was pumping up the dustcart's tyres while Barbara checked over the engine. She'd run her own little car in her teaching days, and had learned the basics of car-maintenance just to save on garage bills. Jenny collapsed, out of breath, and Barbara lowered the bonnet of the dustcart. 'All right, let me take a turn.'

'What's the engine like?'

'Fine as far as I can see. They're usually pretty well maintained in this sort of place. I imagine they used to drive them out occasionally, for parades and exhibitions.'

'Surely the Daleks are bound to hear when we start the engine?'

Barbara stopped pumping, and gave the tyre an experimental kick. 'There, that'll do.' She disconnected the pump. 'We'll just have to chance the noise. It'll still be better than walking.'

Jenny was pessimistic. 'You realise we won't get very far in this old thing?'

'Probably not,' said Barbara patiently. 'But at least it will give us a start out of London.'

'Anyway, do you even know the way to Bedfordshire.'

'Yes, of course ...' Barbara hesitated. 'At least, I used to.'

'What does that mean?'

'Things may have changed. I'm not sure how much damage the Daleks have done.'

'Just wait till you see it,' said Jenny, with a kind of gloomy relish.

Barbara sighed. There were times when she could have wished for a more *cheerful* companion. Once again her thoughts turned to Susan and the Doctor. What were they doing now? And Ian ... What had happened to him?

Crouched in an empty storeroom, Ian and Larry were talking in low voices. Both were tense and watchful. There had recently been a change in the note of the spaceship's engines, and Ian was convinced they would soon be landing. Would they be in Bedfordshire as he hoped? More important, would they be able to get off the ship without being recaptured?

Larry was talking about his missing brother Phil, and his determination to find out what the Daleks were doing. 'Phil got himself sent to the mines on purpose. He reckoned if we knew what the Daleks were doing we'd stand a better chance of defeating them.'

Ian nodded abstractedly, his ears alert for more signs of a landing. 'I suppose that makes good sense.'

'Phil sent back just one message from the mines. He'd worked out some kind of theory ... he reckoned the Daleks were drilling to reach the magnetic core of the Earth ...'

A sudden jolt sent them reeling across the storeroom,

and Ian lost interest in Larry's brother and his theories. 'We're down,' he said excitedly. 'Now—how do we get out of here?'

Larry nodded towards the corner of the room, where there was the usual disposal chute. 'Only one way out. Through there. As soon as we get out, make for cover. I'll go first.'

Larry moved over to the chute, but Ian moved in front of him. 'You realise we've no idea what's out there?'

Larry pushed him aside. 'Only one way to find out.'

He flung open the hatch cover, swung his legs over the edge, and was immediately sucked away by the powerful down-draft. Ian hesitated for a moment. But Larry was right, there was no alternative. They'd never make it down the ramp. He swung his legs over the hatchway and followed Larry. Immediately the suction swept him away. He was whizzing through darkness, sliding down what felt like a giant drain pipe. Suddenly the pipe came to an end and Ian found himself flying through open air. He landed with a thump on solid ground, rolled over on his shoulder and came up running, heading for the shelter of a clump of bushes ahead. He flung himself into the midst of them—and landed on top of Larry, who'd obviously followed exactly the same route.

As soon as he had his breath back, Ian gasped, 'Where do you reckon we are? Is it Bedfordshire?'

Larry parted the bushes. 'Take a look.'

Ian peered through the leaves, and gasped in astonishment. The saucer had landed on what looked like the biggest mining area in the world, an immense muddy valley torn out of what had once been wooded English countryside. It was dotted with mine shaft entrances at regular intervals. There were earth

84

moving machines all around, some of Dalek origin, others obviously commandeered from the humans. Rows and rows of little shacks dotted the site, giving it the air of a mining camp in gold-rush days. A gleaming metal pylon dominated the area, with beside it, a crater like an extinct volcano.

The enormous site was swarming with activity. Slave workers trudged to and fro in long lines, guarded by metal-helmeted Robomen with whips and guns. Here and there Daleks glided up and down on tours of inspection. Ian felt a new respect for Larry's missing brother and his theories. The Daleks were engaged in some colossal undertaking. Surely it held the answer to the mystery of their presence on this planet—and, perhaps, the key to their defeat. He turned to Larry. 'You'll have quite a job, finding your brother in this lot.'

'I'm going to have a darned good try. Come on, let's get on to the site. With any luck we can mingle with the slave workers.'

Making no attempt at concealment, Larry started marching across the site. Ian trudged beside him, hoping they looked like a couple of industrious workers on some errand for the Daleks. They certainly looked as ragged and hungry as the rest of the slaves.

They reached the shelter of a huge excavating machine and paused to survey the activity around them. 'If we can get a chance to grab one of these blokes going by,' whispered Larry, 'we can ask him for news of my brother.'

The familiar hated tones of a Dalek voice rang out. 'Section Beta Zero. Parade for Robotisation selection at hut thirty.'

'I think we ought to find better cover,' muttered Ian. 'There's a bit too much going on round here.'

A voice spoke from behind them. 'And who are you two?' They whirled round. A thin-faced middle-aged man had just come round the other corner of the excavator. He was as ragged-looking as the rest of the slave workers, but at the same time he had an air of natural authority about him. He looked at them impatiently, waiting for their answer.

Larry looked defiantly at him. 'Never mind about us. Who are you?'

'My name's Wells. I'm a section leader. Why aren't you with your work detail? It makes trouble for all of us if you dodge your share of work.' They didn't reply, and he looked more closely at them. 'Escaping, are you? I suppose you know there are Robomen just the other side of this machine?' He reached under the machine and grabbed a pile of picks, tossing some to Ian and Larry. 'Grab these—and leave the talking to me.'

A Roboman appeared round the side of the machine. He stopped, looked searchingly at them and spoke in the familiar slurred voice. 'Who are these two men?'

'I took them from a work detail,' said Wells quickly. 'I needed them to collect more tools.'

'Which work detail?'

Wells waved an arm vaguely. 'I don't know, somewhere over there.'

Ian and Larry stood quite still as the Roboman came closer and looked at them with his dead eyes. 'They must attend for Robotisation.'

Wells shook his head. 'They're needed on their work details. I'll take them back with me.'

'No. They must attend.' The Roboman moved closer to Ian. 'Why do you wait? Move!'

Slowly, very slowly, Ian and Larry began walking away. The Roboman turned to Wells. 'You. Come here.'

86

Slowly Wells walked across to him. As soon as Wells was close enough, the Roboman swung his arm in a brutal arc, clubbing Wells to the ground with the butt of his gun. Wells collapsed face down in the mud, moaning and clutching his head.

Emotionlessly the Roboman said, 'In future, refer all decisions to your masters.'

Ian ran across to Wells and helped him to his feet. After a second's hesitation, Larry ran to join him. Between them they got Wells to his feet, blood streaming from a gash in his forehead.

The Roboman suddenly realised what was going on. 'What are you doing?'

Ian said furiously, 'You can't just leave him like this.'

'Do not disobey orders.'

'Get some other orders!' said Ian contemptuously. Between them Ian and Larry took Wells across to the shelter of the nearest hut.

The Roboman stood quite still, and made no attempt to pursue them.

They laid Wells on the table, and Ian wiped away the blood with his handkerchief. After a moment Wells struggled to sit up. 'I'm O.K. Sorry I got you into that —it was all I could think of.'

'We should be thanking you,' said Ian. He ran over to the window and looked out. The Roboman was still standing quite still. Then he nodded his head abruptly, as if in response to some unheard voice. Gun at the ready, he began marching towards the hut.

The Roboman stepped through the doorway. Wells was sitting on the table, and Larry stood beside him. That was the last thing the Roboman saw. Ian stepped from behind the door and clubbed him down with a savage swing of his pickhandle.

Wells got shakily to his feet. 'We'll have to get out. The Daleks always know when a Roboman is attacked. It cuts off the radio-link. Pick up some tools and try to mingle with one of the working parties. This place is so big there's a chance they'll lose you in the crowd.'

Ian nodded and picked up a couple of picks, passing one to Larry.

'What about you?'

'I know a good hiding place not far away. I've got to stay in the area, I'm meeting Ashton here later.'

'Someone important?' Ian guessed that Wells was one of the leaders of whatever resistance movement existed in the mines.

'Ashton's a rat,' said Wells dispassionately. 'He smuggles in extra food, and sells it to us for whatever we can raise—rings, jewels, anything people have got hidden away. He's useful, though. That extra food has saved quite a few lives.' He looked curiously at Ian. 'I still don't know about you two. Are you trying to break out?'

Ian grinned. 'Believe it or not, we're breaking in. Larry here's looking for his brother, and I'm looking for a friend of mine. I want to take a look around as well, see what the Daleks are up to.'

'You must be mad,' said Wells simply.

'Maybe. Look, whatever happens we'll want to get out of here sooner or later. Will this Ashton smuggle us back to London?'

'Maybe—for a price. Meet me back here when it gets dark—should be safe again by then. I'll tell you what he says.'

Ian shouldered his pick. 'Right, we'll see you later. Come on, Larry, it's time to go down the mine.'

All three slipped quietly out of the hut. They trudged through the mud and attached themselves to a file of slave workers heading towards one of the mine entrances. No one seemed to notice them. Ian guessed that the sheer scale of the enterprise made it impossible for the Daleks to keep tabs on *all* their slaves.

As they headed into the darkness of the mine, Ian suddenly wondered what on earth he was doing. Larry had a definite mission—to find and rescue his brother. But Ian had only the vaguest of plans. First he wanted to look for the Doctor. Knowing the old chap's insatiable curiosity, Ian thought it was a fair bet that the Doctor would come to see what the Daleks were up to. And if he didn't find the Doctor, he'd gather as much useful information as he could, then return to London and take up the search for his companions there. As a scheme it was somewhat on the vague side. But Ian felt a curious sense of excitement as he trudged into the darkness. Somewhere in the depths below lay the secret of the Dalek invasion of Earth. If he could find out what it was, he might yet have a hand in their defeat ...

9

Dangerous Journey

Barbara swung the starting handle of the dustcart. The engine coughed, spluttered, then began to turn over. She withdrew the handle and climbed behind the wheel. Jenny finished flinging back the main doors and jumped in the cab beside her. Slowly the dustcart rumbled out of the museum where it had stood for so many years.

As they came into the street, Jenny glanced briefly at the pile of debris covering Dortmun. A single hand projected from the rubble ... she looked hurriedly away. 'I wonder why he did it?'

Barbara drove cautiously through the empty streets. 'Mostly because he just wouldn't give up.'

'It was senseless,' said Jenny harshly. 'He threw his life away.'

'Depends how you look at it, doesn't it?'

'You've got some romantic idea about this resistance business, haven't you? There's nothing heroic about dying uselessly.'

'Does it occur to you that Dortmun sacrificed himself to save *us*, to draw off the Dalek attack? If he hadn't we probably wouldn't be alive now!'

They drove on in silence for a while. Suddenly Jenny shouted, 'Look out—Dalek!' A Dalek had appeared at the end of one of the side turnings. Barbara put her foot down, and the Dalek disappeared from view as they sped past.

Jenny looked back nervously. 'Do you think it saw us?'

'Even if it didn't it must have heard the noise.'

'Then we're really in for trouble. It'll send a message ahead . . .'

Barbara increased speed. 'We'll worry about that problem when we come to it.'

They came to it very quickly. A turn in the road revealed a line of Daleks stretched across their path. 'What shall we do?' shouted Jenny. 'Jump for it?'

Barbara stamped on the accelerator. 'No! Hold tight, I'm going through!'

Roaring and rattling, the old dustcart sped straight for the line of Daleks, scattering them like skittles. Barbara was vaguely conscious of hitting one head-on, sending it flying through the air. The dustcart lurched as she ran over another one, crushing it beneath the heavy wheels. A Dalek blast sizzled past the open window and then they were through, the line of Daleks scattered in confusion behind them. One or two blasts were fired after them, but Barbara swung the dustcart round a corner and they were safely out of sight. Jenny was bouncing exultantly in her seat. 'We went straight through them, we went straight through them!'

Barbara smiled in satisfaction. 'I enjoyed it too. We can't go on much longer in this thing though. They'll really be after us now.'

On the flight deck of the Dalek spaceship, a message was received from central ground control. 'Rebels travelling north in motorised vehicle. Have broken through Dalek cordon. You will intercept this vehicle and destroy!'

'I obey. Give position of rebel vehicle.' The saucer prepared for take-off.

They were driving along a quiet country lane when suddenly a low droning filled the air. Jenny stuck her head out of the open window and craned her neck to gaze up above. 'It's the Dalek saucer, coming in low!'

Barbara nodded, grim-faced. 'All right. Jump for it Jenny—now! I'll follow you.'

Jenny flung open the door and jumped, rolling over and over on the dusty road. Barbara saw thankfully that the road stretched dead straight ahead of them. She decreased speed slightly, adjusted the steering wheel carefully, then opened her door and jumped clear ... She rolled over as she hit the ground, flinging herself desperately to the side of the road.

High above in the control room of the Dalek ship, a scanner showed the old vehicle trundling along the lane like some bright orange bug. The Dalek commander said, 'Target located. Destroy!' Another Dalek reached out and touched a control ...

A ray shot from the hovering ship and bathed the dustcart in a glow of light. Seconds later it exploded in a cloud of flame and smoke.

The Commander sent a message back to central control. 'The rebel vehicle has been located and destroyed.'

The Dalek ship glided higher and sped on its way back to the mines.

From the roadside ditch, Jenny and Barbara looked regretfully at the blazing remains of the dustcart. Both had jumped clear at the last possible moment. It was Barbara's hope that the Daleks would believe they had died in the flames and call off the hunt. She got to her feet. 'Come on, Jenny, time to move. It's still a long way to Bedfordshire.'

Susan tramped wearily along behind David, wrinkling her nose at the ripe mixture of smells that floated up from the murky waters below. They were following the course of the main sewer, walking along a sort of tow-path beside an underground canal.

'David,' she called. 'Can't we rest for a moment?'

David's heart softened at the weariness in her face. 'Yes, of course we can.'

Susan sank thankfully to the ground. 'How long do we stay down these sewers?'

'Just as long as we can. It's smelly, but its safe!'

Something tinkled by Susan's foot and she held it up. 'Look—a cartridge case.'

David took it and examined it. 'Could be Robomen —though they don't usually come down here.'

'Some of your friends then?'

'Not necessarily. We're not all allies, you know. There are people about who just think of their own survival. They'd kill you for a few scraps of food.' David tapped his rifle. 'This isn't too much use against Daleks, but it will keep anyone else away.'

Suddenly they heard footsteps. A shadow moved down the tunnel towards them. David raised his rifle. 'All right, who are you?'

The shadow stopped. 'David? Is that you? It's me, Tyler.'

David jumped up and ran forward, overjoyed to see his old friend again. Tyler explained that he'd abandoned his search for other guerrilla bands, and decided to go North on his own. 'Did they manage to find that Doctor chap?' he asked.

David nodded. 'He's back there. We left him to rest while we made sure it was all clear ahead!'

'You'd better get back to him. There are renegades about down here, I scared a couple off with this.' Tyler brandished his rifle.

Susan held up the cartridge. 'Did you shoot at one?'

Tyler looked. 'That's mine all right. I wasn't shooting at renegades though.'

'What then?'

'Alligators.' He saw Susan's look of horror and smiled grimly. 'Quite a lot of animals escaped from zoos after the invasion. Most of them died off. But the big reptiles flourished—down here.'

Susan jumped to her feet. 'Come on, David. Let's get back to the Doctor!' She had immediate visions of alligators creeping up to the Doctor's dozing form.

Tyler said, 'Better let me scout ahead, just in case. You two follow.'

David nodded, and Tyler moved away.

Susan called, 'Mr Tyler, you haven't any news of our other friends?'

Tyler said curtly, 'Barbara got back to H.Q. with Dortmun. I left her there—that's all I can tell you.' He disappeared into the darkness. David and Susan waited a few minutes then followed him down the tunnel.

Somehow during their journey he drew further ahead of them, gradually disappearing from sight. They came to a main junction in the tunnels and David stopped. 'This is where we left the Doctor.' He called out, 'Doctor? Tyler?' There was no reply.

'There are these ladders to upper and lower tunnels. Susan pointed. 'Maybe they took one of those.' She moved across to a ladder and began to climb down. 'Mr Tyler? Grandfather, are you down there?'

There was a rusty creaking sound from Susan's ladder. David yelled, 'Be careful,' but he was too late. The top end of the ladder pulled away from the wall and pivoted round on its lower fastening. Susan clung on desperately, and found she was suspended just a few inches over the water. She heard David's voice. 'Hang on! I'll come and get you.' He leaned over, trying to pull her back.

Susan's eyes were fixed on the rushing flood beneath her. Surely there was something moving? To her horror she saw a squat shape gliding nearer. A long jaw lined with savage teeth appeared from the murky water. Susan screamed as the alligator's teeth clashed within inches of her dangling foot.

The alligator dropped back into the water and turned for a second try. Its jaws opened . . .

A bulky shape appeared above her, there was the crack of a rifle. Tyler fired straight into the open mouth of the alligator and it dropped back into the water with a coughing roar. Seconds later Tyler and David had grabbed the ladder and dragged it and Susan back to safety. She collapsed into David's arms. 'Where's Grandfather?'

Tyler pointed upwards. 'Don't worry. I got him to one of the upper levels. It's not really safe down here.'

Susan looked at the murky water and shuddered. 'I believe you.'

David put an arm round her shoulders. 'Don't worry, you'd probably have given the poor old chap indigestion!'

They started to climb the ladder after Tyler.

It lay curled and asleep on one of the throbbing machines. The machine was warm, and it didn't care for the cold on this planet. Suddenly it quivered and woke. Its keen hearing had picked up voices ... human voices. And humans meant food. It slithered from the machine and began sliding quietly through the darkness.

Ian stopped moving and listened intently. 'I tell you I heard something. A sort of slithering noise.'

Larry peered into the darkness. 'Which direction?'

'I'm not sure. It seemed to come from all round ...'

They stood waiting tensely. Their exploration of the mine had not proved a great success. Security was tighter than Ian had imagined, and all the deeper levels were closely guarded. He'd been unable to pick up any real clue as to what was going on here. Nor had they found any trace of the Doctor, or of Larry's brother. Most of their time had been taken up with dodging the constantly patrolling Robomen and their Dalek masters. Now they were back where they'd started, close to the hut where they'd parted from Wells. But this time it was dark—and something very nasty was hunting them through that darkness.

A huge shapeless bulk slithered towards them, making a kind of screaming roar. They jumped back. A Dalek searchlight cut through the darkness, and Ian and Larry flung themselves down. Ian caught a glimpse of a hideous bloated shape, slithering off into the darkness. The searchlight passed by and they picked themselves up. Larry was trembling violently. 'Ian, did you *see*? What was that thing?'

'Search me. Luckily for us it doesn't seem to like the light. Come on, let's get under cover.'

They ran to the little hut and threw themselves inside. Ian closed the door and turned round. Larry was standing absolutely still. From the shadows a man was covering them with a rifle.

96

'Now you can turn round and go out again,' said a cold sneering voice. The man stepped forwards into the moonlight which shone through the window. He wore a soft hat and heavy raincoat, not old and ragged but new and of good quality. His face was round, even a little plump, not gaunt and thin like the slave workers. Suddenly Ian realised who the man was. 'I take it you're Ashton?'

'How do you know that?'

'Wells told us. We came to meet you.'

'You're lying. You came to steal my food. Now get out.' He jerked the rifle barrel towards the door.

Ian didn't move. 'With that thing out there?'

'It didn't see you come in—it needn't see you go out.'

From outside came the roar of the creature that was roaming the darkness. Ian decided he wasn't going outside again whatever happened. The thing was to keep talking. If he could get close enough to jump the man ... Edging a few inches nearer Ashton, Ian said, 'Maybe we can do business together. I want to get back to London.'

'Indeed?' Ashton seemed intrigued. 'And why can't you just die here?'

'I'm not planning to die anywhere yet. I've got friends in London and I want to find them. Can you get me there?'

'Of course I can. For the right price.'

'And what's the right price?'

'As much as you can afford. I'll take anything. Stones, precious metal, jewellery, rings ... I'm not particular ...'

'I'm afraid I don't have very much in that line.'

Ashton smiled coldly. 'Then goodbye. I *do* hope you avoid the Slyther on the way back.'

'We're not leaving.'

'No?' Ashton raised the rifle and worked the bolt. Ian tensed himself to spring . . .

Suddenly the door opened. 'Ashton? It's all right, these two are friends of mine.' Wells slipped into the hut, closing the door behind him.

Ashton lowered his gun. 'You came up with the character references just in time. You've got the goods?'

Wells produced a bundle of objects tied in a handkerchief. He opened it and Ian saw a pathetic collection of wedding rings, cuff-links, ear-rings, bracelets . . . whatever valuables the inmates of the mines had managed to hide. Ashton examined it. 'Not much— but it'll have to do.'

From a corner Ashton produced a small sack, and tossed it across to Wells. 'There you are, then. Now why don't we all have something to eat, boys?'

Wells hefted the sack. 'This has to go round a lot of people. I'll share with my *friends* here—but you're not included, Ashton.'

For a moment Ashton flushed, but he forced a sneering smile back on his face. 'Don't worry. I've brought my own.' He produced a silver hip flask, pushed the top off with his finger and thumb and took a swig. The whole operation was performed one-handed. The other hand still held the rifle, and it was still pointed in their direction.

Ian looked across at Wells. 'Know all the best people, don't you?'

Wells was checking the contents of the sack. 'I told you—he's our only source of real food. You can hardly survive on the slop the Daleks dish out.'

The weird howl echoed through the hut. Ian looked up. 'What is that thing out there?'

'We call it the Slyther. The Black Devil keeps it as a sort of pet.'

'The Black Devil?'

Impatiently Ashton joined in. 'Where've you been —Fairyland? The Black Dalek. Otherwise known as the Dalek Supreme. He's the big boss Dalek.'

'And what's this Slyther thing doing roaming about loose? Is it on guard?'

Wells nodded. 'In a way. There's a curfew, see? The Black Dalek turns the thing loose to deter people from wandering about at night. It wanders round in search of food.'

The howl rang out again. 'What kind of food?' asked Larry nervously.

It was Ashton who answered the question. 'People,' he said simply. 'The Daleks can always spare it a slave or two. They've got plenty more.'

Wells fished out two tins of spam and two tins of peaches, tossing one of each to Ian and Larry. 'Here, we can spare you these. No, don't argue. Take it, you'll need it.' He fished out two tins for himself, and produced a can-opener.

They made a strange, uneasy, meal in the darkened hut, digging the food from the cans with their fingers. Ashton watched them sardonically, taking the occasional swig from his flask. He passed the time checking through the little hoard of jewellery. 'You're a fool, Wells,' he said conversationally. 'There's enough here to buy you a passage out of this place. I could take you to nice empty countryside, plenty of food ... Why don't you forget your ridiculous resistance movement, look after yourself?'

Wells swallowed his last half peach and drained the juice from the can. 'I'll get out ... when everyone gets out.'

99

'Suit yourself. Some people never learn.'

Larry slipped a signet ring from his finger and tossed it to Wells. 'Here, this is for our supper.'

Wells stowed the ring away. 'I'll take it too, if you don't mind. It'll help to buy the next lot from our greedy friend here.'

Whether it was the sound of their voices or the scent of the food they were eating, they never knew, but something led the Slyther to their hut. Suddenly there was a shattering roar and the door burst open. *It* was there filling the doorway. They cowered back as the terrible bulging shape *slithered* towards them ...

10

Trapped in the Depths

Ian saw a vast lumpy blob of a body, powerful flailing tentacles, two tiny deep-set eyes shining with malice . . . Moving incredibly fast, the creature lurched towards them.

It was Ashton who saved their lives, though he was only trying to preserve his own. It was his last good deed, perhaps the only one in his mis-spent life. The rifle was still in his hand, and instinctively he raised it to his shoulder and began blazing away at the Slyther. He succeeded only in attracting its attention. The horrible creature paused for a moment then began rolling swiftly towards him. He fired again and again with no result. Ashton was still screaming when the creature flowed over him and engulfed him entirely.

Ian didn't like to leave even Ashton to the mercy of the Slyther, but it was dreadfully clear that there was nothing they could do for him. 'Quick,' he yelled. 'Now's our chance.' Leaving the Slyther to its feast, Ian, Larry and Wells ran from the hut into the darkness outside. Immediately they were caught in the beam of a Dalek searchlight. 'Scatter!' yelled Wells, and they all split up, Wells running one way, Larry and Ian the other. From behind them came the screaming roar of the Slyther as it abandoned Ashton to pursue the rest of its prey.

Ian and Larry struggled to the surface of a low mound of earth. In its centre was a crude mine shaft, a deep round hole. A wooden derrick straddled the hole, and from the derrick hung an enormous iron bucket, obviously designed for carrying earth.

They paused, wondering whether to run round the excavation or go back—when the Slyther appeared over the top of the mound, rushing towards them at amazing speed.

Ian acted without thinking. He took a flying leap through the air, clutched the side of the earth-bucket and scrambled inside. Larry hesitated, took a look at the approaching Slyther, and followed his example. Ian grabbed him and hauled him inside the bucket.

Howling with rage the Slyther ranged to and fro on top of the mound, its prey just out of reach. 'It's still after us,' shouted Ian. 'I hope it can't jump!'

Larry grabbed Ian's arm. 'It's going to try!'

Larry was right. The Slyther somehow *gathered* itself, then flew through the air in a tremendous leap. It landed on the edge of the bucket and began scrambling over the side.

Terrified by the thought of being trapped inside the bucket with the voracious monster, Ian and Larry fought like demons. They heaved and kicked and punched at the Slyther's flabby bulk, shoving it out of the bucket with maniacal fury, dodging the flailing blows from its enormous tentacles. A last desperate heave sent it over the edge. With a long final scream, the monster disappeared. There was a squelching thud as it struck the edge of the crater, then screaming in rage and pain it slithered off into the darkness ...

For a moment Ian and Larry crouched in the bucket, panting for breath. Then Larry gasped, 'Come on, let's get out of here.' He started to climb the side of the bucket, but Ian held him back. 'No—someone's bound to have heard all that racket. Let's just stay here till things quieten down.'

In the mine control room deep below the surface, a Dalek engineer was studying his work-chart. He turned to his assistant, 'There is no work party in shaft nine. Why?'

The assistant consulted another chart. 'The section is completed. A labour force is now being assembled for clearing operations.'

'Work must proceed to schedule. There must be no delay.'

'All will be ready. I shall now lower the waste bucket into shaft nine.' The assistant touched a control.

Ian listened cautiously. Everything seemed silent. 'It's all clear now.'

'Might as well take a chance,' agreed Larry. 'Can't stay here all night.'

There was a shuddering, a clanking sound—and Ian and Larry felt the bucket jerk into sudden movement. 'What's happening?' yelled Larry.

'Hold tight,' shouted Ian. 'We're going down!' And so they were. Slowly the bucket clanked down into the darkness below.

'I must say this is a nice state of affairs,' announced the Doctor peevishly. 'All this time and we're still hiding in sewers.'

David grinned, well used to the Doctor by now. 'Better to hide down here, Doctor, than be caught by the Robomen. As soon as Tyler says the coast is clear we can travel on the surface again.'

They had climbed up from the deeper parts of the sewer system and were now in a stone walled antechamber directly below street level. A ladder led up through a manhole, and Tyler had just gone ahead to see if it was safe for the rest of them to emerge.

There was a scrambling sound and Tyler shot down the ladder, rifle in hand. Susan looked up hopefully. 'Is it clear?'

'It is *not*,' announced Tyler grimly. 'Ran straight into a patrol. I couldn't get under cover, they came after me.'

David grabbed his rifle. 'How many?'

'Just two of them.'

Tyler started back up the ladder. 'David and I will deal with them, you stay under cover.'

'Just a moment,' said the Doctor mildly. 'Wouldn't it be better to—er, lure them down here? If they succeeded in communicating with their fellows and summoning reinforcements ...

Tyler shook his head ruefully. 'I suppose if we stick together long enough I'll learn to do what you say the first time. All right, David, you draw them in. Don't shoot unless you have to, ricochets might get one of us.'

David climbed up the ladder, emerged through the manhole, and ran a little way into the street. The Robomen saw him immediately and wheeled round in pursuit. They raised their guns, but David had already disappeared down the manhole.

Crouched in the corner of the little chamber, the Doctor and Susan waited. David and Tyler were also waiting, one each side of the ladder. The first Roboman came to the top of the ladder, paused, then slowly began to descend. As soon as he was down, Tyler grabbed him round the throat and pulled him to the floor.

The second Roboman more cautious, paused halfway down the ladder. David grabbed his feet and pulled him down. The two men collapsed in a wildly struggling heap. The Roboman's gun went off, but luckily the shot went up through the open hatchway.

Quickly David raised his rifle and used the butt to club the Roboman into unconsciousness.

The Doctor went over to Tyler, who was methodically choking the life out of his victim. 'That will do, Tyler,' he said sharply. 'I never countenance the taking of life unless my own is directly threatened.' The astonished Tyler let go of the Roboman who slumped unconscious to the floor. The Doctor made his way to the ladder. 'Now then, let's be on our way to this mine, and then we shall discover how to deal with the Daleks. We'll leave these poor creatures to their own devices. David, you lead the way, my boy. Come along, everybody.' Very much in command, the Doctor bustled his party up the ladder.

Barbara and Jenny were tired and footsore by the time they came to the little cottage in the forest. It was nearly dark now, and there was an ominous rumbling in the sky, with occasional lightning flashes. They'd cut across country, keeping off the roads for greater safety, but now night was coming and they were lost somewhere in thick woods.

Jenny looked at the cottage. 'It seems deserted. What do you think, shall we try it?'

Barbara hesitated. There was something sinister about the tumbledown old cottage. It looked curiously like the witch's house in some fairy tale. She told herself she was being over-imaginative. 'Well, there's a storm coming on. We'd be much better off under shelter.'

They moved cautiously up to the front door. Suddenly it swung open and a hag-like old woman dressed in rags stood glaring at them, a lantern held over her head. Jenny jumped back with a scream, and Barbara thought wildly that perhaps it was a witch's house after all . . .

The old woman snarled, 'What do you want?'

Barbara made her voice calm and reassuring. 'We're lost. We were looking for shelter.'

'Just the two of you?' The old woman gave a sudden cackle of a laugh. 'Tired are you?'

'Yes . . . yes, we are.'

Jenny looked at the old woman uneasily, 'Barbara, I think we should be moving on.'

The smaller, equally ragged figure of a younger woman appeared beside the first in the doorway.

'Dogs'll get you,' it piped suddenly.

'Dogs?' Barbara echoed nervously.

The old woman took up the chorus. 'Terrible beasts. After the plague they formed a pack. They hunt travellers. You'd better come in.'

Reluctantly Barbara and Jenny stepped inside. The cottage was dirty and primitive, like something out of the Middle Ages. A bed, a stove, a ricketty table and some battered wooden chairs were all the furniture of its single room. Barbara looked at the two women who stood nodding and smiling. It was clear from their close resemblance that they were mother and daughter. Barbara told herself that she was wrong to feel repelled by them. They were poor and ignorant that was all, and small wonder in this horrible world the Daleks had made. 'Where are you making for?' asked the old woman suddenly.

Barbara sank into a chair, suddenly realising how tired she was. 'The Dalek mines. We have friends there. We're trying to find them.'

The younger woman shook her head dolefully. 'Nobody ever gets away from the mines. You'll be caught yourselves.'

The old woman nodded. 'You're lucky you got this far—and found us. Patrols pass here all the time.'

Jenny was still suspicious. 'Then how is it you're still free. They must know you're here.'

The old woman cackled. 'Oh, they know all right. But we can't harm them.'

'We helps 'em,' piped up the younger one.

The old woman scowled at her, swiftly changing to a smile as she turned back to Barbara. 'We make clothes for the slave workers,' she explained. 'We're more use to them doing that than we would be in the mines.'

'How do you manage for food?'

'They give us a bit from time to time, payment you might say. We go hungry most days though.'

Even Jenny was won over by their sad faces. 'We've got a little food with us,' she said gruffly. 'You can share it if you like.'

The old woman gave a toothless grin. 'Why thank you, my child. We've little to offer in return, but if you like you can sleep here for the night. We can make up a bed in that corner, you'll be comfy enough.'

There was another rumble of thunder, and rain began lashing down. Barbara realised she couldn't face going out again. 'Thank you,' she said wearily. 'We'll stay the night if we may.'

Jenny unpacked the meagre supplies—apples, a tin of meat, some rather stale biscuits. The old woman put out some plates, four battered tin mugs and a jug of water.

Barbara noticed that the younger woman was wrapping herself in a heavy hooded cloak. 'Where are you going?' she demanded.

'I have to go out to deliver these clothes.'

'In this weather?'

The old woman sighed. 'Daleks don't care about the

weather, my dear. We have to keep up our quota—and these are late already.'

'What about those dogs you told us about?' asked Jenny.

'She follows the patrols,' explained the old woman.

The younger nodded eagerly. 'That's right, I follow the patrols.'

'She'll come to no harm,' said the old woman soothingly. 'She's done it often enough before. Now why don't we sit down and enjoy our meal? The girl will have hers when she gets back.'

Jenny shared out their food with scrupulous fairness, putting aside a portion for the younger woman, and they sat down to eat.

Barbara and Jenny ate the scanty meal in tired silence, but, the old woman was excited and talkative. She plied Barbara with questions about London. 'What's it like now, dearie, still as wonderful?'

'I'm afraid not. The Daleks have destroyed quite a lot of it.'

'Destroyed? Well I never! When I went it was all *so* pretty. The shops and the moving pavements ... and I went to the Astronauts' Fair ...'

The old woman rambled on about her once-in-a-lifetime day trip to London, and all the wonderful things she'd seen. Barbara's head began nodding. It was pathetic really, she thought, she should feel sorry for the poor old thing. But somehow she still felt uneasy. The old woman was nervous too, glancing constantly at an old alarm clock on a shelf, and looking out of the window. Probably worrying about her daughter.

Suddenly bright light flooded into the room as the clearing outside was lit up with a blazing searchlight. Jenny screamed as the cottage door smashed open. In the doorway stood a Dalek, flanked by Robomen guards. 'Both of you will follow me. Do not try to escape or you will be exterminated!'

Stunned, Barbara and Jenny stood up, and gathered their few possessions. How had the Daleks found them so easily? The thin figure of the daughter dodged round the Dalek and scuttled to her mother's side. She held out a little sack. 'Look, ma. There's bread, and oranges and sugar ...'

The old woman chuckled. 'Good, good. I knew they'd give us food if we told them.'

Impatiently the Dalek shouted, 'Move!' As Barbara and Jenny were marched out of the cottage, the other two women were excitedly rummaging through the sack. The older one looked out of the window as the Robomen led their captives away. 'Such a pity,' she muttered. 'Still, they'd have been captured anyway, in the end.' Eagerly she sucked the juice from her orange. She hadn't tasted an orange for years and years ...

The giant wastebucket clanked down through the darkness on a seemingly endless journey, taking its human cargo deeper and deeper into the Dalek mine. Ian supposed he shouldn't complain, since he'd wanted to get into the mine anyway. But he hadn't bargained for travelling this way. He heard Larry's nervous voice from the darkness beside him. 'How long do you think we've been going down now?'

'Must be nearly twenty minutes.'

'It's getting warmer, isn't it?'

'Yes ... pressure's increasing too, my ears are popping.'

Larry shuddered. 'I'd rather be dead than work down here.'

'I hope we don't have to make the choice!'

'We're stopping,' said Larry excitedly. 'We must be nearly at the bottom.' He craned his head over the side of the bucket. 'Look—lights, just below!'

Ian saw a huge open space, the junction of several earth-walled tunnels supported by wooden pit props, lit by dim working-lights. Piles of earth and rock were everywhere. 'Let's get out of here, before this bucket tips over and chucks us out.'

They clambered on to the rim of the giant bucket. This was by no means an easy job, since the bucket tended to tip with the movement of their weight. Ian wriggled over the edge, hung by his hands and dropped. The fall was a long one, but he landed unhurt in a pile of soft earth.

Larry wasn't so lucky. He landed with a thud right beside Ian, but when he tried to get up he groaned and clutched his leg. 'It's my knee. I hit it on the bucket coming down.'

Ian looked round. 'We must hide for a bit till you can walk. It's too open here. Come on, put your weight on me.'

He helped Larry away from the open area and into one of the side tunnels. They crouched in the semi-darkness, resting thankfully.

After a few minutes Ian said, 'How's the leg?'

Larry straightened it, and gave another groan. 'Seems to be stiffening up. I don't think I'll be able to walk.'

'Don't worry. We'll stay here for a while.' Ian looked out of the tunnel and into the main area. There were lots of tunnels leading off, enormous piles of earth and stones, and that was all. 'This mine doesn't make sense to me. All they seem to be digging is rocks. I suppose they could be processing ore somewhere.'

'You remember what my brother Phil said—the Daleks want to tunnel through to the magnetic core of the Earth.'

'But why? What are they up to?'

Larry shrugged. 'You can't tell much from here. This is only a sort of clearance area. Perhaps the important work's going on somewhere else.'

'You may be right at that.' Ian felt a surge of impatience. It was maddening to be so close to the Daleks' secrets without learning more. 'Larry, would you be all right if I went to have a look around?'

'Yes, sure.'

Ian got to his feet and moved out of the tunnel into the main area. He chose the largest of the tunnels leading off, and made his way along it. Soon he heard voices and movement coming towards him, and ducked behind a pit prop for cover. Cautiously he peered out. A procession of gaunt ragged men and women was stumbling along the tunnel, driven by the whips of Robomen guards. They clutched a variety of containers, and some carried picks and shovels. Ian turned and ran back to Larry.

'Lay low and keep quiet. There's a crowd of workers and Robomen coming this way.'

Larry and Ian watched from hiding as the workers flooded into the central area. The huge bucket in which they'd travelled down suddenly dropped the rest of the distance to the ground, tipping over on its side. Immediately workers began carrying earth and rocks from the piles and tipping them into the bucket. They worked at a feverish pace and the whips of the Robomen lashed out at anyone who slowed down or stumbled.

A Roboman spoke briefly to one of the slaves who

collected a small group of workers. The Roboman started leading them across the area and into the tunnel in which Ian and Larry were hiding ... Gun in hand, he marched straight towards them ...

11

Action Underground

A few yards from Larry and Ian, the Roboman halted his party, and set them to work on the nearest rock-pile.

Ian put his lips to Larry's ear and whispered, 'We'll have to move back! They're clearing this whole section ...'

Desperation gave Larry the power to overcome the pain in his twisted knee. Ian helped him to his feet and they started edging their way deeper into the tunnel.

Larry's foot slipped, and he fell back against the tunnel wall with a moan of pain. The Roboman left his workers and ran towards them, covering them with his gun. 'Halt!'

Ian and Larry stood quite still. The Roboman stared intently at them. Ian guessed that the Robotising process reduced the human mind to the lowest level, capable of giving and receiving only the simplest of commands. Finally the Roboman worked things out. 'You are not in the working party. Who are you?'

Larry gripped Ian's arm in a painful grip. 'It's Phil,' he whispered. 'Ian, it's my brother Phil.' He moved closer to the Roboman, staring into his face. 'Think, Phil. You must remember me. I'm your brother, Larry. *Remember me!*'

There was no change in the Roboman's voice or expression. With the same painful slowness, he came to another conclusion. 'You are runaways.'

'Angela,' said Larry desperately. 'Remember your wife, Angela. I can take you to her.'

'You must both be punished. I shall take you to the Daleks. Follow me.'

The Roboman turned, taking obedience for granted —and immediately Ian jumped him. The Roboman fired at once but Ian shoved the gun barrel upwards and the blast hit the ceiling. They wrestled fiercely for possession of the weapon. Once again Ian realised the inhuman strength of the Robomen, their total imperviousness to pain.

Helplessly Larry watched Ian and the Roboman roll over and over, finishing up almost at his feet. His back to Larry, the Roboman wrenched free of Ian and stood up. He levelled the gun at Ian's still prone body—and with a scream of 'No, Phil, no!' Larry launched himself at his brother's back, ripping the Roboman helmet from his head ...

The gun exploded again, missing Ian and bringing rock down from the wall. The Roboman screamed and convulsed, collapsing in his death agony. Sobbing Larry held the body in his arms. He knew he hadn't really killed his brother. The Daleks had done that a long time ago, when they'd taken away his humanity.

Stunned and shocked, Ian scrambled to his feet. Larry was still clutching Phil's body, tears streaming down his face. Behind them in the main area an alarm signal was ringing out, and there was a confused shouting.

'Come on, Larry, run!' shouted Ian. 'Here, I'll help you ...'

Larry shook his head. 'You run, Ian, while you've got the chance. They'd only get both of us ...'

From the tunnel behind them came a voice shouting 'Halt!' A Dalek was at the end of the tunnel, a Roboman behind him. Ian flung himself to one side and the Roboman fired a long raking blast. Larry's body jerked convulsively, and he collapsed on top of his dead brother. Ian turned and ran into the darkness of the tunnel. Behind him he could hear the Dalek's blaring voice. 'Emergency, emergency in shaft nine. Seal all exits! Emergency!' Ian ran blindly on into the darkness.

The Doctor stood on a wooded hill overlooking the Dalek mineworkings, his face solemn. He studied the shafts, the machinery, the immense ordered pattern of activity for a moment longer, then turned to his companion. 'Thank you, Mr Tyler, I've seen all I need to see.' They turned and made their way back through the wood.

As they walked back to their little camp, the Doctor mused how often there seemed to come a period of tranquillity in the time of greatest danger. After their fight with the Robomen in the sewer, they'd had a surprisingly peaceful journey to Bedfordshire. They'd even travelled by road for a part of the way in an abandoned car that Tyler had managed to get working.

It was certainly an idyllic scene that met them as they returned to the camp. They'd established themselves by a little stream, and David had produced fishing gear from his pack and started to fish. Clearly he'd been successful, for Susan was frying trout over a small fire, while David himself could be seen coming downstream with another fine fish in his hand.

The Doctor watched smiling as David crept up behind Susan and suddenly thrust the fish over her shoulder. Susan screamed and jumped up. David caught her in his arms, and kissed her. Astonished, Susan stood quite still. The Doctor cleared his throat very loudly, and made a deliberate crashing noise as he came through the bushes.

The two young people jumped apart and David babbled, 'Ah, yes, there you are, Doctor. We were, that is, I was just ...'

The Doctor looked at the sizzling frying pan. 'Yes, I could see something was cooking,' he said dryly. He looked closely at Susan. How deeply was she involved with this young man? For some time now the Doctor had been aware that Susan was fast growing up, and that their wandering way of life posed problems that would one day have to be faced ... Still, time enough for that later on. First they had to solve the problem of the Daleks. Unless *that* was dealt with, they'd none of them have a future to worry about.

The meal was the most enjoyable one they'd had in quite some time, and the Doctor's instincts told him it might be even longer before they got another. The food was simple enough, fish, biscuits, the remains of their tinned fruit. Tyler even produced some long-hoarded coffee from his pack. It was jet black, milkless and sugarless, but still delicious.

As they sat round sipping it, David asked, 'Now you've actually seen the Dalek base, Doctor, what do you think?'

'Well, young man, it's quite obvious to me that these mine workings are the centre of their entire operations.' He gave Tyler a reproving glare. 'I really can't think why you didn't focus all your resistance efforts down here.'

Tyler grunted. 'That's all very well, Doctor. We've been fighting the Daleks wherever we could. Fighting to stay alive mostly!'

David came to his support. 'We assumed they were just mining for Earth's minerals, looting the planet.'

'No,' said the Doctor decisively. 'These workings hold the answer to the one question that is of any importance to you. *Why* are the Daleks here?'

David looked puzzled. 'Why? Surely they're here because they've invaded us? It's as simple as that.'

'Indeed it isn't, young man. It goes much deeper. The Daleks have no interest in Man as such. He's just a work machine, an insignificant specimen of life scarcely worth conquering. It doesn't *matter* to the Daleks whether you live or die.'

'All right,' said David. 'Suppose you're right, Doctor. What *are* the Daleks up to?'

'I'm not quite sure yet, my boy. There must be something about this planet, something no other planet can offer. It's nothing near the surface, or they'd have collected it and gone. Instead there they are, burrowing like metal moles, deep into the Earth's crust!'

Tyler scratched his head. 'I'm no scientist, Doctor, but surely ... if they penetrate the Earth's crust they'll cause an enormous earthquake—something nobody will survive?'

'That is so—unless they've found some way of controlling the flow of living energy.' The Doctor looked round the little group. 'The Daleks are daring to tamper with the forces of creation—and we must dare to stop them!'

There was a moment of silence. The Doctor's words had made them all aware of the tremendous issues they were facing.

Suddenly the Doctor stood up. 'Time to pack up camp and be on our way,' he ordered. 'We have a great deal to do.' No one questioned the order. Once again, the Doctor had taken charge.

Ian ran on through the darkness until he saw a glimmer of light ahead. He slowed down and went more carefully. The tunnel widened ahead, and joined up with several others. Rows of slave workers were filling their buckets and emptying them into wheeled trucks, which others pushed away. Robomen stood on guard and occasionally a Dalek moved past. It all looked very familiar, and suddenly Ian realised why. He'd stumbled upon another clearing area, a point where the endless debris from the Dalek's drilling was collected and hauled to the surface. Ian looked along the line of workers. A tall, dark-haired woman was emptying a bucket of rocks. Ian gave a silent gasp of astonishment. It was Barbara. He started creeping nearer ...

Barbara and Jenny had been toiling for hours now, and Jenny was beginning to crack up. She was carrying yet another basket of rocks to the wastebucket when she stumbled and fell, spilling most of the painfully gathered rocks. She crouched by the overturned basket, almost sobbing with despair. 'It's no good, Barbara, we're beaten. We'll never get out of here, never.'

Barbara knelt to help her. 'Steady, Jenny, that's no way to talk. We wanted to get to the mine and here we are.'

'But there's nothing we can *do*.'

'We can get this bucket filled for a start,' said Barbara practically.

Already a whip-carrying Roboman was moving towards their part of the mine. 'Move,' he shouted. 'Continue with your task.'

Barbara went on tossing rocks into the basket. 'We can try to find their main control room. That's what the Doctor would do.'

Jenny sniffed. 'And what do we do then?'

'I don't know, Jenny, but at least we could try to do *something*. If we don't succeed, we'll just end up back here.'

From his hiding place nearby, Ian saw one of the Robomen address a crouched over slave worker. 'You! Collect more containers from the nearest storage section.'

The man straightened up, and started moving towards Ian. To his joy he saw it was Wells, the man who'd helped him and Larry earlier. As Wells passed his hiding place Ian hissed softly. 'Wells, it's me, Ian.'

Wells pretended to have trouble with his shoe, bent to fix it. 'Ian? Should have thought you'd have been out of here by now.'

'That tall girl over there—I know her. See if you can get a chance to speak to her. Tell her I'm here.'

Wells picked up the last bucket. 'I'll try. But I've got to get the buckets first.' He trudged off along the tunnel and Ian settled down to wait for his return.

On the work line, Jenny was still objecting. 'They'll never let us get *near* their control room.'

Something crackled inside Barbara's coat as she bent down for another rock. 'Jenny, I've just realised. I've still got Dortmun's notes.'

'A lot of use they are!'

Barbara suddenly lost patience with Jenny's pessimism. It was time to act. A Dalek was coming towards them. Deliberately Barbara straightened up and stepped out in front of it. The Dalek stopped, eye-stalk swivelling round in astonishment. 'Continue work.'

Barbara stood her ground. 'I have important information for you. Rebels are planning a revolution against the Daleks.'

The Dalek's reaction was immediate. 'There will be no revolution. The Daleks are masters of Earth.'

'You don't understand. This is no ordinary uprising. They have scientists working with them.'

'You are lying. It is a trick.'

'No. I have proof.' Barbara held out Dortmun's notes.

The Dalek scanned the first page. 'These contain details of the acid bomb used in the unsuccessful attack on the Dalek spaceship.'

'There's more,' said Barbara quickly. 'We know the names of the rebels, the places where they plan to attack.'

'You will tell me immediately.'

Barbara shook her head. 'No, I must speak to someone in authority. You'll have to act at once on what I tell you, and it's all very complicated.'

The Dalek paused, considering. Barbara held her breath. Then the Dalek spoke. 'Very well. I will take you both to the Dalek Supreme. If you are lying you will be killed. Follow me.'

The Dalek set off down the tunnel, Jenny and Barbara following behind.

Ian watched all this from hiding, not really understanding what was going on. Wells came back down the tunnel, loaded with buckets. 'All right. Take some buckets, and follow me. I'll try to get you to your friend.'

'Too late. The Daleks have just taken her off.'

'They've probably taken her to the control room for questioning.'

'Then that's where I'm going. Just you point me in the right direction. Come on! Give me some of those buckets.'

Ian stepped out boldly behind Wells, and walked along the line of workers handing out buckets. The Robomen didn't seem to notice him. Wells took him to the far end of the line and pointed. 'That tunnel at the end there, runs towards the control area. Good luck.'

Wells turned back towards the line of workers, and Ian ran off down the tunnel.

Very soon the nature of the tunnel started to alter. Earth and rock walls gave way to metal. There was better lighting and the hum of powerful machinery nearby.

At the end of the tunnel was an open door, and through it Ian could see a long room lined with banks of strange machinery and complex control panels. Daleks glided to and fro, tending the instruments. Ian crept quietly to the door and slipped inside.

The place was so enormous, the Dalek scientists so absorbed in their many tasks, that Ian found it easy to slip from machine to machine and work his way to the centre of the area. He saw no sign of Barbara. What he did see was a circular hole in the centre of the area, about the size of a large well. From the concentration of Daleks and instruments around this spot, something very important was going on. Ian crept closer, looking for a good hiding place, near enough to allow him to eavesdrop.

Facing him, and just on the edge of the area was a curious container, rather like half of a giant metal egg. Cables ran into its top. It was partly filled with machinery, but there was just room for Ian to duck inside and crouch down out of sight. He was near enough now to hear the voices of the Daleks as they moved busily around their instruments.

He saw the Daleks in the group wheel round as a large Black Dalek approached. 'Give me your report.'

'The main drills have penetrated the final strata. We are within four miles of the Earth's outer core.'

'When will final breakthrough occur?'

'As soon as the slave workers have finished clearing the top of the fissure, we shall put into position the penetration explosive. The charge is already prepared in the capsule.'

The Black Dalek addressed those around it, rather like a professor delivering a lecture to students. 'The charge will be timed to detonate in the fissure in the Earth's crust. The fissure will expand and the molten core will be released. We will then control the flow until all the gravitational and magnetic forces in the Earth's core are eliminated. I shall now announce to Dalek Earthforce the near completion of Project Degravitate.'

The Black Dalek moved across to a communications console.

Ian listened eagerly. He had arrived at a crucial moment, just as the secret of the Daleks' plans was to be revealed. He heard the voice of the Black Dalek once more, this time echoing through a whole series of loudspeakers. Clearly the announcement was being relayed over the entire control area.

'This is the Supreme Controller. Our mission to Earth is nearly completed. We were sent here to remove the core of this planet. Once the core is removed we shall replace it with a power system. This will enable us to pilot the planet anywhere in the Universe. All that remains is to put into position the penetration explosive capsule. Daleks controlling this device will now report.'

There came another voice. 'The device is ready.'

'Capsule to closed position.'

Inside his hiding place, Ian's mind was reeling at the sheer audacity of the Dalek plan. To steal an entire planet, to steer it around the Universe as a moving base for conquest ... No doubt something about the structure of the Earth had made it exactly the kind of planet the Daleks needed. They weren't taking anything *from* Earth—they were stealing Earth itself!

Lost in thought, it took Ian a moment too long to notice that something was happening. The container in which he had hidden was gliding across the floor. Another identical metal shape, its opposite half, was moving towards it. The two halves clicked together to form a giant metal egg, shutting Ian inside.

The capsule glided across the control room floor until it was suspended above the central well. The overhead cable was paid out and the container slowly descended into the bomb-shaft.

The Black Dalek's voice rang out in triumph. 'Once the capsule has been guided into position, it will be released. It will travel to the fissure in Earth's crust and then explode.'

The penetration explosive capsule was on its way— and Ian was trapped inside.

12

Rebellion!

Inside the capsule Ian was struggling frantically. The metal container was completely sealed, the only possible exit a small hatch in one side. Ian set his back against one side of the capsule and kicked frantically at the hatch with his heels. The capsule swung violently to and fro on the end of its cable.

Suddenly it jerked to a halt.

In the control room above there was pandemonium. A panic-stricken Dalek scientist reported, 'Capsule oscillating violently, due to operation of unknown forces. Descension mechanism has ceased to function.'

The Black Dalek was in a fury. 'Recover capsule and re-check immediately.'

'Descension mechanism now jammed. Capsule must be drawn up manually. Alert Robomen working party. Emergency!'

Soon the capsule began moving upwards again, more slowly now, as a party of sweating Robomen heaved on the cable. It was still spinning to and fro as Ian inside kicked frantically at the hatch.

In the control room a Dalek scientist announced. 'Capsule now arrived at sub-station immediately below this level. Still vibrating violently.'

The Black Dalek decided to take no chances. 'Arrest capsule at sub-station. Ascertain cause of breakdown.'

The capsule jerked to a halt, just as Ian finally kicked the hatchway open. He peered out of the hatch. He was at a point where an intersecting tunnel cut at right angles across the vertical shaft. Down that tunnel a Dalek was speeding straight towards him.

Ian jumped from the capsule and looked round for an escape. There was only one way to go—down.

A coil of rope lay amidst a jumble of timbers at the edge of the shaft. Ian tied the rope round a pit prop, threw the other end into the shaft and started climbing down.

The Dalek arrived at the shaft and spun round angrily, puzzled by the disappearance of its prey. Then its eye-stalk swivelled on to the knotted rope. It fired at the beam and the rope blazed and snapped in two ...

Ian began whizzing down the smooth metal shaft, scrabbling desperately at the sides. The edge of another tunnel intersection flashed by and he flung himself forward frantically. He hit the edge with an impact that drove the breath from his body. Painfully, Ian pulled himself up into the lower tunnel. With the last of his strength, he crawled slowly away into the darkness. Halfway down the tunnel he slumped forward, unconscious.

Barbara and Jenny heard the Dalek Supreme's announcement while they were waiting in the outer control area. Like Ian they were astonished at the scope of the Dalek scheme. Soon they were taken to the centre of the control area and ordered to wait until the Black Dalek was free. It was clear by the number of Daleks bustling about, and their evident agitation, that there was some kind of crisis.

Barbara looked curiously at the opening to the bomb shaft. No doubt this was where the penetration capsule had been lowered. She whispered to Jenny, 'See if you can get to one of the control panels and do some damage. I'll try to hold their attention.'

She could hear agitated Dalek voices. 'Dalek unit reports human being discovered in capsule. Human fell down bomb shaft in attempt to escape.'

The Black Dalek was still issuing orders. 'Every error must be corrected. The penetration explosive *must* strike the fissure correctly if we are to extract the molten core. Are all slave worker tasks completed?'

'Only final clearance remains.'

'Once clearance is completed, you will confine all slave workers below ground level. When the molten core breaks through they will be completely exterminated.'

Completely unmoved by this order to commit mass murder, the aide moved to the communications console. 'To all Robomen. Herd all human slaves to lower galleries as soon as clearance is complete!'

Jenny looked at Barbara in horror. 'Did you hear what they're planning to do?'

Barbara was thinking furiously. 'That's where they control the Robomen ...'

'Maybe we can put it out of action,' said Jenny eagerly.

'Better than that—we can use it.'

A Dalek guard ordered them forward, driving them to stand before the Black Dalek. 'Here are the humans who reported an imminent revolt.'

The Black Dalek scanned them. 'Speak!'

Barbara held out Dortmun's notes. 'This is the bomb——'

'We are not interested in the bomb. Give information on planned revolt.'

Barbara racked her brains for a sufficiently colourful story. 'Well, it's planned to start quite suddenly, like the Indian Mutiny.'

'We have already conquered India.'

Barbara rattled on, ignoring the interruption. 'I'm talking about Red Indians of course, in disguise, like the Boston Tea Party. General Lee and the Fifth Cavalry will attack from the North while Hannibal's forces move in from the Southern Alps . . .'

While the bemused Daleks were listening to this historical mish-mash, Jenny made a sudden dash for the communications console. Immediately a nearby Roboman grabbed her—but the diversion gave Barbara *her* chance. She ran to the console. 'Attention all Robomen. You will attack the Daleks. Attack the Daleks——'

Like a huge metal dodgem car, the Black Dalek shoved Barbara aside. 'Cancel last order. Resume normal operations.'

The order given, the Black Dalek swung menacingly towards Barbara and Jenny. An aide came forward, 'They were lying to trick us. Shall I exterminate them?'

The Black Dalek considered for a moment. 'No. Hold them here for interrogation. I will deal with them later. There is still much to be done!' Moving to the communications console, the Black Dalek began issuing a further stream of orders.

'Spaceship will hover above main crater, ready to evacuate all Dalek personnel. Repair capsule and descension mechanism. Return capsule to main control . . .'

As they were marched away, Barbara whispered, 'Sorry, Jenny.'

'What for? It was a marvellous try—and it nearly worked.'

Their Roboman guard shouted, 'Silence!' Robomen smartly grabbed Barbara and Jenny and manacled them to clamps on a nearby pillar. All around the bustle of Dalek activity continued.

At the edge of an enormous crater, David and Susan were waiting while Tyler and the Doctor crawled round the rim of the excavation.

'Any idea what they're up to?' asked David.

Susan shook her head. 'The Doctor never explains anything. He'll tell us when he's ready.'

David sighed. 'Well whatever it is, I just hope it works. The Doctor seems to be our only hope.' He paused. 'Susan—if we are successful—what will you do?'

'Go on travelling with grandfather, I suppose, moving from place to place ...'

'Wouldn't you *like* to belong somewhere? Like here —with me?'

Susan looked at him in distress. 'Please, David, don't ask me that. I just don't know.' She looked at his unhappy face. 'I'm sorry, David, really ...'

They moved apart as the Doctor and Tyler came back to them. The Doctor rubbed his hands together briskly. 'David, my boy, have you any of those bombs left?'

'Just three, I think.'

'That will be sufficient. Now, you see that radio-mast over there with the cables leading away? I want you and Susan to destroy it. Use the bombs, you can detonate them from a distance with your gun. Off you go —and don't stop to pick flowers on the way.'

As David and Susan scrambled away, the Doctor turned to Tyler. 'I don't think they'll run into any trouble—but I can't say the same for us! We're going down this crater. Come along!'

The Doctor started scrambling rapidly down the steeply sloping sides. Tyler shook his head in reluctant admiration, and started climbing after him.

Ian was never sure how long he'd been unconscious but it couldn't have been very long. He came to, suddenly, in the darkness of the lower tunnel, his mind still full of the Daleks' terrible plan. If there was only something he could do to frustrate them ... He had just one advantage. He was still very close to the shaft down which the bomb capsule must pass. If he could only stop or divert it ...

Ian walked slowly back along the tunnel to the bomb shaft. He peered upwards, to where the light shone down from the Dalek control room. They'd hauled the bomb-capsule back up by now. Soon they'd have it repaired, and ready to drop. Released from its cable it would plummet down the bomb shaft, into the fissure and then explode. Unless ...

Just as there had been on the level above, there was a pile of timber close to the end of the tunnel. Ian looked thoughtfully at the heavy planks. Heaving and struggling, he dragged a plank off its pile and laid it like a bridge right across the bomb shaft. He pulled out another plank, and another ... Some time later, his work completed, Ian ran back up the tunnel. He was looking for a way through to the upper levels. If his plan worked, the tunnel he was in now would soon be a very unhealthy place.

Tyler and the Doctor stood by a massive metal door let into the side of a tunnel. The Doctor was rubbing his chin. 'Since it isn't *guarded*, there's probably a photo-electric alarm ...'

He examined the lower edge of the door. 'Ah yes, here ... and here. One to trigger the alarms, one to open the door. Now, I need something shiny.'

Tyler produced his knife. 'Will this do?'

'Excellent.' Using the shiny blade of the knife as a mirror, the Doctor reflected the light beam of one cell into the other. 'By glancing one beam on to the other, we open the door and neutralise the warning system ... so!' There was a crackle of electricity, a shower of sparks and the door sprang open.

Tyler scratched his head. 'I'll say one thing, Doctor, life with you is never dull!' They passed into the Dalek Base.

Manacled and helpless in the control room, Barbara and Jenny watched as the re-checked capsule was swung out over the bomb shaft. The Dalek Supreme ordered, 'Commence lowering capsule!'

The huge metal egg, this time without a human passenger, was lowered slowly down to the bomb shaft.

The Dalek scientist moved to a control. 'Am releasing capsule—now!'

(The penetration explosive capsule dropped only a short distance further down the bomb shaft, before it hit the wooden barrier constructed by Ian. Deflected from its intended path, the capsule rolled down the side-tunnel, hit the earth wall, then stopped, hidden in the darkness.)

Proudly the Black Dalek announced 'The Capsule is on its way to the core of this planet. When it reaches its destination it will detonate automatically. We shall go to the edge of the mine workings for greater safety. We shall remain in the Dalek spaceship until we are certain it is safe to return. All Daleks will now evacuate this base.'

Barbara gave Jenny an agonised glance. The Dalek plan looked like succeeding after all. And they were being left behind—to die.

13

Explosion!

Tyler and the Doctor jumped back into an intersection, as a long line of Daleks moved down the corridor ahead of them. Tyler popped his head out. 'That was a near one.'

The Doctor nodded. 'They seem to be on the move. Let's go to where they've come from.'

Jenny and Barbara were still struggling with their manacles when Tyler and the Doctor made their way into the now deserted control area. The reunion was excited and ecstatic. 'My poor Barbara,' said the Doctor indignantly. 'Mr Tyler, help me get these things off.' Tyler set to work on the manacle locks with his knife, and soon Barbara and Jenny were free again.

Briefly Barbara explained what she'd gathered about the Daleks' plan. The Doctor seemed unsurprised. 'I thought it would be something like that. I'm working on a scheme to circumvent them. Now, let me see if I can work this scanner.'

The Doctor swiftly adjusted controls and a little screen in front of him sprung to life. It showed various shots of the mines, then suddenly a picture of Susan and David laying bombs around the base of an enormous radio mast. 'They're trying to blow up the mast and so fracture the outer cable ring,' explained the Doctor.

Jenny was none the wiser. 'What good will that do?'

'You know the Daleks communicate by a sort of radio network? Well, if the radio-link is suddenly broken it will give them a most tremendous shock. A kind of brainstorm. It should immobilise them completely, at least for a while ...'

A Dalek voice crackled from a nearby speaker. 'Interference to scanner settings in main control area. One Dalek unit will return to investigate!'

Tyler ran to the doorway. 'There's a Dalek coming along the corridor now!'

On the screen David and Susan continued their task with maddening slowness.

From the doorway Tyler called, 'Doctor—the Dalek's nearly here!'

He ran back to join them at the scanner. Seconds later a Dalek glided into the control area.

The Doctor stood quietly at the scanner, ignoring the approaching Dalek completely.

On the screen they saw David and Susan finish laying their charges, and retreat to a safe distance. David raised the rifle to his shoulder, then a flash filled the screen. When it cleared they saw the radio mast toppling slowly to the ground.

The Doctor beamed triumphantly, turned round—and saw the Dalek heading straight towards him.

Tyler tried to pull him aside. 'Run, Doctor, it hasn't worked.'

The Doctor shook him off, and stepped directly in front of the Dalek, hands clutching his lapels.

The Dalek said, 'Halt! Who *aaare* ...'

Its voice seemed to wind down, and trail away into silence. The Dalek stopped moving.

Tyler gave a huge sigh of relief. 'You certainly took a chance.'

'Science, my dear chap, not chance. It took a little time for the effect to be felt, that's all.

'What will you do now, Doctor, stop the bomb?'

After this latest display, Tyler was quite prepared to believe the Doctor could do anything.

'All in good time,' replied the Doctor calmly. 'I'm not sure how long this little shock will hold the Daleks. We must find some more permanent way of dealing with them.'

Barbara said excitedly, 'The Robomen, Doctor. That console controls them. I tried ordering them to attack the Daleks, but they caught us. Let me try again.'

The Doctor gave an assenting wave of his hand and Barbara rushed to the console. 'Robomen, this order cannot be countermanded. Attack the Daleks! Destroy them!'

The Doctor stepped up to the console. 'Slave workers —here is your freedom. Use it. Destroy the Daleks.' He turned away from the console, rubbing his hands with glee. 'Now come along all of you. Let's see what happens!'

They walked along the corridor towards the mining area. Soon they heard a clamour and a shouting, the ringing of metal on metal. They turned a corner to find a seething mob of slave workers and Robomen battering and smashing at a Dalek with pails and picks, until it was no more than a hunk of twisted metal. The crowd rushed past them, obviously searching for more Daleks to destroy.

A grimy ragged figure dashed out of the crowd and caught Barbara in his arms, hugging her till she was breathless. 'Ian,' she cried delightedly. 'Ian!'

'Bless my soul, it's young Chesterton!' said the Doctor. 'Where did you spring from, my boy?'

Ian shook the Doctor's hand like a pump handle. 'Doctor! I might have guessed you were behind all this. Just listen to them!'

From all over the mine came the sound of exultant

shouting, the roar and clamour of battle. The Doctor smiled. 'The people of Earth are fighting back at last.'

They made their way back to the control room, exchanging a babble of congratulations, explanations and recitals of all their different adventures.

The Doctor listened gravely as Ian told of his attempt to deflect the bomb. Ian crossed to a chart on the wall which showed the bomb shaft plunging down to join the fissure in the Earth's crust. He put his finger on the chart. 'If the contraption works, the bomb's jammed here—just a couple of levels below us.'

'A brave scheme, my boy,' said the Doctor, 'But not without its perils to the rest of us. The bomb won't release the Earth's core as the Daleks had hoped. But there will be the most tremendous explosion in a very short time!'

'How long have we got, Doctor?'

The Doctor crossed to the bomb control area. 'If I read these dials correctly—something in the order of ten more minutes!'

Barbara ran to his side. 'Can you switch it off to delay the explosion?'

The Doctor shook his head. 'The bomb was intended to explode deep within the Earth's core, remember. The detonation device is automatic—and self-contained.'

'Then we've got to get out of here!' said Tyler urgently. 'And we've got to get everyone else out too!'

The Doctor went over to the communications console. 'The public address system will still be working. It's on a separate circuit.' He cleared his throat and spoke into it. 'Robomen and slave workers. This mine is about to explode. You must make for the surface and leave the area immediately. Never mind the Daleks. Leave them to their fate. I repeat, this mine is about to explode. Leave the area immediately.' He turned to the others. 'We've done all we can. It's time to look to our own safety. Follow me. We'll go out the way I came in!'

Swiftly the Doctor led them out of the control area along the corridors, out into the tunnel, and finally in a last frantic scramble up the sloping sides of the crater. They found Susan and David waiting for them at the top. 'Don't talk—run!' ordered the Doctor breathlessly, as they joined the crowds fleeing desperately from the mine.

They witnessed the end of the Dalek invasion of Earth from the hill overlooking the mine area. The place looked like a disturbed ant-hill, long lines of people streaming away from it in all directions. The Dalek spaceship hovered over the main crater, but made no attempt to attack, waiting no doubt for the results of the experiment.

As the last few escapers fled from the mine there was a low subterranean rumble ... It grew steadily until, suddenly, the whole of the mine workings erupted in a great belching cloud of smoke and flame. The noise was shattering, and they all dropped to the ground, hands over their ears. All except the Doctor, who stood watching the holocaust with keen scientific interest.

The incredible noise ended at last, dying down to a low, constant rumble. They looked up to see a huge mountain of earth, the crater on its top belching smoke and flame. 'Quite a sight, eh, Mr Tyler,' said the Doctor. 'An active volcano in England!'

Jenny looked upwards. 'What happened to the Dalek spaceship?'

'Totally destroyed,' said the Doctor with satisfaction. 'I saw it. They were caught in the first up-blast of the explosion.'

Jenny stood looking at the sky. Barbara put an arm round her shoulders. 'It's all right, Jenny, it's over ...'

'Over,' said Jenny quietly. Barbara saw tears streaming down her cheeks. Suddenly she realised—in all their adventures together, it was the first time she'd ever seen Jenny cry.

14

The Farewell

It took them a very long time to make their way back to London, the riverside, and the building-site where the TARDIS had been trapped so long ago. So many people wanted to congratulate them, to hear the story of their adventures and final triumph. But they arrived at last, and now the Doctor stood looking on in quiet satisfaction while a willing gang of Tyler's men cleared the last of the girders away from the TARDIS door.

London was already a very different place from the ruined city in which they'd arrived. There were people in the streets again and even a few cars, and boats on the river. Everywhere was a spirit of hope, the sense of life starting again. London was being reborn before their eyes.

Tyler stood beside the Doctor and looked round at the bustling scene. 'It's a pity Dortmun isn't here to see this. Dortmun and lots of others like him.'

'It's up to you to build their memorial,' said the Doctor quietly. 'A new London, a better Earth. I'm certain you'll succeed.'

The TARDIS was clear at last. Tyler nodded towards it. 'There's your police box, Doctor. And I won't ask questions. As far as I'm concerned you're welcome to every police box in London.'

The Doctor smiled. 'This one will do, thank you.' A sound rang out, a sound once familiar to every Londoner, one that had been missing for a very long time—the chimes of Big Ben. Tyler smiled content-edly.

The Doctor left him listening happily to the chimes, and scrambled down to Susan. She was sitting on a beam of timber, absently toying with her TARDIS key, which hung as usual on a chain around her neck. 'All alone, child?' he asked gently.

Susan smiled. 'I've already let Barbara and Ian into the ship. I was just—thinking.'

The Doctor sat down beside her. 'Hasn't been much time for that recently. I'm afraid you must blame me— I seem to have a nose for trouble.'

Susan gave him an affectionate hug. 'You know I wouldn't blame you for anything, Grandfather.'

They sat in silence for a while. Several times the Doctor seemed about to speak, and then changed his mind. Susan seemed plunged in a fit of abstraction. Suddenly she stood up and said, 'Ah well——' then broke off, wincing.

The Doctor jumped up too. 'Susan, you're hurt ...'

Susan stood on one foot. 'No, I'm all right. I just trod on a sharp stone.' She held up one shoe to reveal a gaping hole in the bottom. 'The journey to the mines wore them out completely.'

The Doctor took the shoe from her, pursing his lips. 'Dear me. Still it's nothing to worry about. I'll soon mend it for you.'

Susan smiled at him affectionately. The funny thing was that he was quite serious. It was typical of the Doctor that he was quite as willing, and as able, to repair a worn-out shoe as he was a damaged spaceship computer. 'It's all right, Doctor, I've got plenty more pairs in the TARDIS.'

The Doctor frowned. 'That reminds me, I'd better

go and check up on the ship.' He gave Susan a pat on the head and wandered off, the shoe clutched in his hand.

Susan was still sitting on the beam when David came quietly up to her. He sat beside her, his arm round her shoulders.

'Susan, stay with me,' he pleaded.

'David, I can't! I don't belong on your world or in your time.'

'I love you, Susan. I'm asking you to marry me.'

'I have to stay with grandfather. He's old now, he needs me. Please—don't ask me to choose between you.'

David took a deep breath. 'You told me once you'd never really belonged anywhere. That's what I'm offering you now, Susan. A place and a time of your own.'

Susan stood up and started limping towards the TARDIS. There were tears in her eyes. 'Goodbye, David. I'm all right. I just trod on a nail.' She limped off towards the waiting police box. As she moved away she said quietly to herself 'But I do love you, David. I do ...'

The Doctor stood at the TARDIS console, still holding Susan's shoe. Behind him Ian and Barbara stood hand in hand. They knew the dilemma the Doctor was facing, but there was nothing they could do to help.

Suddenly the Doctor stood very erect. He put Susan's shoe down carefully, reached for a particular control-switch and slammed it over, hard.

Susan had almost reached the TARDIS when its door closed in her face. She took the key from round her neck and tried to open it. Nothing happened. 'Grandfather,' she screamed. 'Grandfather!'

Suddenly she heard the Doctor's voice. 'Susan, please listen. I've safety-locked the door—you can't get in.'

Inside the TARDIS the Doctor could see Susan's

puzzled face looking at him on the scanner. Gently he said, 'All these years I've been taking care of you—and all the time, you really felt you were taking care of me ...'

He heard Susan's voice. 'But I belong with you ...'

'Not any more, Susan. Your future is with young David, not with an old buffer like me.' He saw that David had come to join Susan, his arm around her. 'Look after her, David, my boy. Be kind. Work hard both of you. You'll find that life on Earth can be an adventure too.'

For a moment the Doctor's voice faltered, then he recovered himself. 'Now then, both of you, no regrets. And look to the future. Remember, both of you, love's the thing. That's what really counts. Goodbye. One day I'll come back. One day ... Goodbye ...'

Susan and David stepped back, as the dematerialisation noise began, and the TARDIS disappeared.

Quietly David said, 'He knew, Susan. He knew you could never leave him. That's why he left you.'

As David took Susan in his arms the TARDIS key slipped from her fingers, and lay unregarded on the ground. Susan made no attempt to pick it up because she knew she wouldn't be needing it again.

Inside the TARDIS the Doctor turned away from the scanner with a sniff. He glared at Ian and Barbara, as if daring them to comment. When they said nothing, his face broke into a smile. 'I'll get over it,' he said briskly. 'Bound to happen one day. Now then, I really must get you two home again. Right place *and* the right time, eh? Let's see what we can do!'

As the Doctor leaned over the console, his fingers moving over the controls, Ian gave Barbara a nudge. 'I wonder where the old boy will land us up this time!'

'I'd be willing to bet you it's not Earth,' she whispered.

Through the Space Time Vortex, the TARDIS sped on its way. The Doctor still had two faithful companions, and many more adventures lay before them.

ANIMAL STORIES

Judith M. Berrisford
0426107004	**SKIPPER AND SON**	(illus)	35p
0426107195	**SKIPPER AND THE RUNAWAY BOY**	(illus)	35p
0426104870	**SKIPPER – THE DOG FROM THE SEA**	(illus)	30p
0426107276	**SKIPPER'S EXCITING SUMMER**		40p
0426104951	**SKIPPER TO THE RESCUE!**	(illus)	30p

Molly Burkett
0426111567	**THAT MAD, BAD BADGER . . .**	(NF)	35p

Ernestine N. Byrd
0426100654	**ICE KING**	(illus)	25p

Constance Taber Colby
0426109899	**A SKUNK IN THE FAMILY**	(illus) (NF)	45p

G. D. Griffiths
0426113675	**ABANDONED!**	(illus)	35p

Sara Herbert
0426109627	**THE PONY PLOT**		35p
0426109708	**THE SECRET OF THE MISSING FOAL**		35p

Alex Lea
0426107861	**TEMBA DAWN, MY CALF**		30p

Joyce Stranger
42611017X	**THE SECRET HERDS**	(illus)	45p

Alison Thomas
0426115511	**BENJI**		40p

'DOCTOR WHO'

Terrance Dicks
426114558	**DOCTOR WHO AND THE ABOMINABLE SNOWMEN**	(illus)	40p
426112954	**DOCTOR WHO AND THE AUTON INVASION**	(illus)	40p

Malcolm Hulke
42611471X	**DOCTOR WHO AND THE CAVE MONSTERS**	(Illus)	40p

David Whitaker
426113160	**DOCTOR WHO AND THE CRUSADERS**	(illus)	40p

Brian Hayles
426114981	**DOCTOR WHO AND THE CURSE OF PELADON**	(illus)	40p

Gerry Davis
426114639	**DOCTOR WHO AND THE CYBERMEN**	(illus)	40p

Wyndham Books are available from many booksellers and newsagents. If you have any difficulty please send purchase price plus postage on the scale below to:

Wyndham Cash Sales,
123 King Street,
London W6 9JG

OR

Star Book Service,
G.P.O. Box 29,
Douglas,
Isle of Man,
British Isles

While every effort is made to keep prices low, it is sometimes necessary to increase prices at short notice. Wyndham Books reserve the right to show new retail prices on covers which may differ from those advertised in the text or elsewhere.

U.K. & Eire
One book 15p plus 7p per copy for each additional book ordered to a maximum charge of 57p.

Other Countries
Rates available on request.

N.B. These charges are subject to Post Office charge fluctuations.